AMONG THE LIVING

PSYCOP 1

AMONG THE LIVING

a PSYCOP novella

Jordan Castillo Price

PSYCOP 1

jCPBOOKS.com

Standalone print edition published in the
United States in 2016 by JCP Books
www.jcpbooks.com

First Standalone Print Edition

ISBN-13 978-1-935540-83-0

Cover art by Jordan Castillo Price

Audio edition available

Once upon a time if you told doctors you heard voices, they'd diagnose you as schizophrenic, put you on heavy drugs, and lock you away in a cozy state institution to keep you from hurting yourself or others.

Nowadays they test you first to see if you're psychic.

Maurice was a sixty-two year old black man who had a lot more gray in his hair at his retirement party than he'd had when I first met him. We'd never been close in a way that some partners at the Fifth Precinct are. We didn't hit sports bars after our shift for a shot and a beer. We didn't watch the game at each others' houses. We didn't invite each other to family functions—not that I have any family to speak of.

Maybe it was the race difference. Or the age difference. But despite the fact that we didn't connect on any sort of deep, soul-searching level, I was gonna miss working with the guy.

I stood behind the kitchen island and watched through the glass doors that led to the deck as Maurice ambled by. He laughed as he tried to balance a Coors Light, a styrofoam tray of bratwurst and a small stack of CDs. He looked genuinely happy. I supposed he was ready to retire—not like those guys you hear about that are forced out, along with all of their years of honed experience, in favor of some young buck who'll work for half the salary.

Maurice set the CDs in a sloppy, listing pile next to a tinny boom box and drained his beer in one pull. I wondered if being retired would entice him into a long slide down the neck of a bottle, but then I felt a little guilty for even thinking it. Because Maurice never, ever made comments about my Auracel—whether I had taken any, or was out, or was rebounding after a weekend of "accidentally" doubling or tripling my dosage. Nothing.

Maybe that was the actual reason I was gonna miss him so much.

I turned away from the deck and made my way back down the hall, and tried to remember where the bathroom was. I veered accidentally into the rec room and a bunch of black kids, mostly teenagers, all fell silent. I nodded at them and wondered if I'd managed to look friendly or if I just came off as some creepy, white asshole, then headed toward the basement where I remembered there was a half bath off Maurice's seldom-used woodshop.

"That's him, Victor Bayne," one of the kids whispered, so loud that it was audible to my physical ears. Not that my sixth sense would've picked it up, given that I was pretty far into a nice Auracel haze, and besides, I wasn't particularly clairaudient. "He was my dad's partner on the Spook Squad."

I quelled the urge to go back into the rec room and tell Maurice's kid that his dad would probably shit a brick if he heard that expression in his home. But that'd lead to a long-winded discussion of civil rights, yadda yadda yadda. Plus I'd be absolutely certain to come off as a creepy, white asshole then, in case there was any doubt at all.

I groped around the cellar wall at the top of the stairs for several long moments for a light until I realized the lights downstairs were already on. I made a mental note to rib Maurice about the availability of light bulbs greater than 40 watts come Monday. Except Maurice wasn't gonna be there on Monday. Damn.

My eyes adjusted and I took the cellar steps two by two. I imagined what Maurice's kid was probably saying about me to his cousins and friends. It was pretty plain that I was the psychic half of the Maurice/Victor team, since Maurice was about as psychic as a brick wall, and damn proud of it.

A pair of opposites forms a Paranormal Investigation Unit. The Psychs—psychic cops—do the psychic stuff, just like you'd expect. And the Stiffs—look, I didn't name 'em—are oblivious to any psychic interference a sixth-sensory gifted criminal might throw out there. It was rough at first getting used to riding around with a guy who put out about as many vibes as a day-old ham sandwich. But I got used to it, and eventually I grew to see the practicality of pairing us with each other.

Halfway down the steps I reached into my jeans pocket and found a tab of Auracel among the old gum wrappers and lint. I felt around some more, but only managed to locate the one. I'd brought three with me. Had I taken two earlier? I only remembered taking one in the car. Oh, and there was the one I took when Sergeant Warwick came in. The irony. Popping pills within spitting distance of someone capable of cutting off my precious supply.

I swallowed the Auracel, grabbed hold of the bathroom door and barely caught myself from slamming face first into Detective Jacob Marks, the golden child of the Twelfth Precinct Sex Crimes Unit.

He was a big, dark-eyed, dark-haired hunk of a guy with a neatly clipped goatee and short hair that looked like he had it trimmed every single week. He'd always looked beefy to me from afar, standing in the background, tall and proud, as his sergeant praised his work on high profile cases during press releases while the cameras flashed and the video rolled. But up close it was obvious that he was as wide as two of me put together, and it was all solid muscle.

I think I excused myself and staggered back a step or two. The Auracel I'd taken on the stairs was stuck to the roof of my mouth and I swallowed hard, worried that its innocuous gelatin coating would dissolve and give me a big jolt of something bitter and nasty. The Auracel didn't budge.

"So," Marks said, deftly swerving his bulging pecs around my shoulder as he maneuvered past me. I stood there gaping and trying not to choke. "Lost your Stiff."

A comment about the crassness of calling Maurice a Stiff stuck somewhere around the last Auracel, as I realized that Marks not only knew who I was and what I did, but that he seemed to be flirting with me. Detective Marks—queer? Who knew? And besides, he was a Stiff, too.

Or maybe he was just a jerk and the flirting notion was merely something that my mind constructed from the high it'd gleaned from two Auracels and a few fumes.

I shrugged and raised my eyebrow. Nothing like being noncommittal. Especially when I only had access to five senses, and even those were pretty fuzzy around the edges.

Marks leaned back against Maurice's workbench and crossed his arms over his chest. That pose made him triple my diameter, and his tight black T-shirt was stretched so taut over his biceps that it probably wanted to surrender. "New partner lined up yet?"

I wondered if "partner" was also supposed to be flirtatious, as in "sexual partner." But even my Auracel-addled mind figured that'd be a pretty far stretch. I had nowhere to lean, so I stuffed my hands in my jeans pockets and hunched a little, as kids who are taller than their classmates tend to do. Marks was as tall as I was. I like that in a man. "It's all hush-hush," I said, belatedly thankful that I didn't make a tongue twister out of those last couple of words. "I think they had like a hundred applicants."

Marks cocked his head to one side, considering me. The bitterness of Auracel spread over the back of my tongue and I swallowed convulsively—smooth move. "Probably more like a thousand," Marks said, "but they screen ninety percent of them out before the interviews start."

A thousand people wanted to be the Stiff half of a Paranormal Investigation Unit—homicide, no less? I imagined I'd be flattered, if I weren't choking.

I stifled a cough and dry-swallowed three, four more times. My eyelashes felt damp.

And Jacob Marks had pushed off from the workbench and pressed right up against me. "What's in your mouth?" he said, and his voice was a sexy, low purr. He pulled my face up against his, pried my mouth open with his and skimmed his tongue across the inside of my upper lip. "Auracel? Isn't that the strongest anti-psyactive they make?"

How would he know what Auracel tastes like? I probably would've asked him myself, except I wasn't quite fit for speaking. Or even breathing, for that matter. I squeezed my hand up between us and managed to push back from Marks before I hurled all over him. The bathroom sink was only a yard away, and I turned both taps on, scooped up tepid water with both hands, and struggled to dislodge the pill from my soft palate.

Finally, the foul thing tore free and made its way down my throat. It felt like it'd left behind a chemical burn on the roof of my mouth and the back of my tongue. I cupped a few more handfuls of water from the tap, drank them, and then splashed one on my face for good measure.

I stared down at the sink as the water dripped from my hairline. Cripes. Jacob Marks kissed me, sorta, and I was too busy choking on a pill to get into it. I assumed I'd just blown a perfectly good shot at some hot, nearly-anonymous sex when I heard Marks' voice again coming from the doorway. Apparently I hadn't succeeded in scaring him off. His reflection met my eye in the medicine cabinet mirror.

"One in every five hundred people is certifiably psychic, and they're all clamoring for something to shut their talent off. What kind of sense does that make?" he asked. There was a friendly lilt to his tone of voice, but the look in his eye made his words feel like more of a challenge.

Well, didn't he know his facts and figures? I ran my hand up through my half-wet hair. The mirror reflected it back at me. It stood up in a crazy, black thatch. I needed a haircut.

I flipped open the door to see if maybe there was some Listerine in there to wash away the taste of the Auracel, but found nothing but a bottle of Jergen's lotion and a few yellowed aspirin left over from the Reagan Era.

"You're a PsyCop." I turned to face Marks. "Why don't you ask your partner?"

"Carolyn's all natural," he said. And I wondered if they were fucking each other, though

I guessed it was really none of my business.

I think his prying would normally have pissed me off. But I'm not normally three Auracel to the wind, so I played along. "Good for Carolyn," I said. "Do dead people like to talk with Carolyn? All day, all night? Describe how they died? In excruciating detail?"

"Carolyn can tell if people are lying."

"A human polygraph," I said, and I supposed it was clever. You didn't need someone's consent to use your psychic ability, not if you had a federal license. But you did need a court order to hook someone up to a lie detector. "No wonder you collar so many perverts."

Marks broke into a smile that was almost more of a leer, and I realized he was probably a lot more fun than I'd ever imagined he'd be. "It helps," he said. "But Carolyn's only a level two, and criminals can be incredibly evasive." He pushed the bathroom door shut with his foot and locked it behind us. The tiny doorknob twist lock seemed pathetically inadequate, considering that any cop upstairs could kick the door in without even breaking a sweat, but maybe the sanctity of the bathroom would protect us from discovery.

Marks eased up to me and then stopped, that infuriating—yet sexy—grin plastered on his face, framed by his impossibly neat goatee. I wondered what he wanted. More witty repartee? The third Auracel was kicking in and I hardly had two brain cells to rub together, so I closed the distance between us, slipped my arms around his neck and initiated a kiss of my own.

His tongue tasted beery, but pleasantly so, like he'd just had a drink or two at the party. I wished I could drink, but while alcohol loosens me up just like anyone else, it also amps up the voices. I don't drink.

He got a hand around my waist and slipped the other around the back of my jeans, kneading my ass hard, showing me his strength. I grazed his lower lip with my teeth and he grunted a little into my mouth, ground his fly against mine.

Marks backed me into the towel rack, which settled right beneath my shoulder blades, and started kissing me hard, rubbing up against me while his sweet tongue swept over my bitter one.

I was the one to fumble with buttons and zippers, to expose our stiff cocks to the ambient light of my ex-partner's bathroom. Marks seemed pleased enough to let our experience take him where it would and to have me call the shots. But then again, Marks could probably pick people up whenever he was horny. I had to jump on any chance that presented itself to me and hope I was on Auracel—or at least able to get my hands on some. I really hate threesomes when one of the participants is dead.

Marks had a thick, fat cock, rock hard and ruddy. Mine had a certain delicacy and grace beside his as he took them both in his hands and pumped them, hard, even strokes, while I cupped his jaw between my palms and languidly tongued his mouth.

He knows, I thought, and though his grip was harder than I might have liked, my body still responded to it, thighs clenching and warmth building at the base of my spine. He knows who I am. And he knows what I do. And he's willing to jack me off anyway.

I trailed my fingertips over his scalp, through his closely-shorn hair, and he groaned into my mouth, his hands moving faster on us. My breath hissed in and I caressed the tips of his ears and the curve of his jaw with a feathery touch. I sucked on his tongue.

He pulled back to watch himself as he came, his jiz rolling down over his knuckles as he clenched his cock hard, and I suddenly liked his face a whole lot better. Open like that, and vulnerable. Not the handsome, self-assured detective who always got his man, but just a guy jacking off with me. His mouth was so pretty—a little swollen now, from kissing me. I imagined it closing around the head of my cock, taking me into its soft, wet warmth, and then my hips gave a twitch and I was coming. It was a pretty energetic spurt, given the amount of drugs in my system, and the first rope of come managed to paint itself down the front of Marks' T-shirt and across the leg of his black jeans.

I sniggered a little as I shot again, more weakly though, just over his bare forearm, and again. Marks stared at me, our sticky cocks loose in his grip, and then he broke into a big grin, too. My vision was going all starry around the edges and I was glad of the towel rack behind me, and the big cop in front of me. I still had my arms draped over his shoulders, and couldn't think of any good reason to let go.

Someone banged on the door. "Bayne? You in there?"

I pressed my forehead into Marks' shoulder and exhaled carefully. I could've ignored it, if it was anyone else but Sergeant Warwick. But that voice, in that tone, would need to be answered. "Yeah, Sarge."

Marks gave my cock a slow, teasing stroke. It gave up a final bead of semen.

"I need you at the station. Now."

On a Sunday? When we were all at a party, some of us drunk, some of us pill-buffered, and some of us getting lucky? Whatever it was, it wouldn't be pretty. "Okay," I said. I considered dropping something into the toilet to make it sound like I was taking a big dump, but then I'd either have to fish the object back out or leave it in there to screw up Maurice's plumbing. Instead, I tugged at the toilet paper roll and tried to make it rattle. "I'll be out in a minute."

We both listened to Warwick's footsteps as he headed back upstairs. Marks' face had shifted back into cop-mode, his shrewd, dark eyes scanning the empty air in front of him as he analyzed whatever theories he was assembling inside his head. "Something big just went down." He pulled a yard of toilet paper from the roll and wiped my jiz off his leg.

Chapter 2

Sergeant Warwick was a square, middle-aged man with a thick neck. His graying blond hair was thinning on top, but at least he had the decency not to subject us all to a bad comb-over. He sat behind his clunky metal desk, rolling a pen between his thumb and forefinger like he did every time something really pissed him off. "Bayne, this is your new partner, Lisa Gutierrez. She's worked homicide four years now, in Las Vegas and Albuquerque. Gutierrez, Victor Bayne."

Lisa Gutierrez looked as Latina as she sounded, her long, dark hair pulled back from her fresh-scrubbed, no-makeup face so hard it almost made my head hurt to look at it. She was young, mid-twenties, and my guess was that she'd been a uniformed cop in her previous job. She must have done something extraordinarily special to land her current assignment—a job that a thousand other people lost out on, at least according to Marks.

I tried to look really focused as I shook her hand, but maybe I was just kinda making my pale blue eyes bug out at her instead. Three frigging Auracels, three, not even counting the one I'd had the night before, and the whole world seemed like it was made out of cotton candy with some interesting sprinkles thrown in for shits and grins. I'd come right over from the party and I hoped to God I didn't smell like sex. I thought our encounter was brief and furtive enough that I probably didn't. I considered taking up smoking to cover any inappropriate smells I might someday harbor. I didn't necessarily have to inhale if I didn't want to.

"Are you medicated?" Warwick said. Because it's so professional to accuse someone of being high right as you introduce them to their new partner. It's some kind of newfangled team-building exercise, all the rage in L.A.

"I was at my partner's retirement party," I snapped, deciding I would have to admit to one Auracel, but not three. They couldn't prove I'd taken three without a really expensive and time-consuming drug test. "What do you think, I wanted that idiot who hung herself in his garage to follow me around the whole afternoon? That's my idea of a great party, lemme tell you."

Warwick twirled the pen harder while his

jaw worked. "Detective Bayne is authorized, when he's off duty, for the use of Auracel..." he started to explain.

"An anti-psyactive," said Gutierrez. "I know what it is. Now tell me what's so unusual about this case that you'd call Bayne in instead of assigning it to the team on call."

Warwick blinked, and then pulled out a manila folder, opened it, scanned the contents and began gathering his thoughts. I stuck my hand in my pocket in order to stop myself from giving Gutierrez a high-five, since she seemed so clipped and professional that she'd probably leave me waving in the wind. But damn, I liked her.

I was happy to let Gutierrez drive since I was legally impaired, although a breathalyzer wouldn't have been able to pick up on it. She was just in from Albuquerque and didn't have a car yet, so we took mine. She had to move the seat up three whole clicks.

"That was...um...cool," I said as I got into the car, wondering if I could possibly sound any more retarded. "The way you got Warwick off my case."

She glanced at me. "Your pupils are totally dilated. You should put on some sunglasses before you damage your retinas."

Maybe she was genuinely concerned, or maybe she wasn't so lax on the whole drug thing after all. She had that deadpan delivery that was kind of hard to read. I rummaged around my glove compartment and found an old pair of shades crusted with mysterious dust. How did things get dusty while they were shut inside a glovebox? I also saw half a tab of Auracel cradled inside the hinge. I took a pen and flicked it out to stop it from being crushed when I closed the door, and then moved my registration over to cover it up. Gutierrez' eyes were on the tiny GPS navigation screen. Also dusty, I noted.

"It'd be faster if you turned up Clark," I said.

Gutierrez ignored my directions, preferring instead to trust the Magellan. She'd turned the audio down, but still glanced at the map occasionally.

"Were you a PsyCop at your last job?" I asked.

A little smile played on her lips, and she was actually kinda cute in that moment, like a kid sister. "They don't even have 'em in New Mexico." She pronounced Mexico with an "X" in the middle, like I would. I wondered if the "Me-HEE-co" pronunciation was reserved for the country.

We passed Clark again, a diagonal street that defied the grid of the rest of the city, and I sighed. "Then how'd you land this job? Not that I'm complaining, but I heard the competition was pretty...fierce." I wondered if she thought I was crass enough to say "stiff."

Gutierrez shrugged and turned on Lawrence. Her jacket didn't quite fit her in the shoulders. She was petite and a little stocky, would probably need something tailored. I wondered how I knew that, given that I owned only two sportcoats and my sloppy dress shirts were about twenty years out of style. I figured it was the Auracel thinking for me. And then I realized I was still in jeans, a big no-no given the department's dress code. That's what they got for calling me away from a party on the opposite side of the city from my apartment.

"My track record's good," she said. "Beyond good. And besides," she gave me a sly look. "I count as two minorities: a woman and a Hispanic. Your boss's got his quotas to fill, just like everybody."

I stared through my dusty plastic lenses at a string of Indian grocers and sari shops and noted that I could kind of see over one lens but not the other. Therefore, the shades were probably crooked as well as dusty. Charming. "Our boss." I tried to straighten out the glasses and failed.

The Magellan beeped as Gutierrez missed a turn onto Artesian and then readjusted itself to plot her a new course to the scene. I figured she must've been sightseeing and just passed it by.

"The Auracel," she said, taking the next right, "it works for you?"

"It makes the dead people shut up," I told her. And, by golly, the high was just an added bonus. I didn't tell her that. Oh, and it only muffled the ambient dead people. If I really, really wanted to, I could try real hard, pick one out and make him spill his guts. But I didn't mention that, either. A guy's gotta have some boundaries.

She nodded and pulled up behind a pair of squad cars. I glanced down Artesian and saw a pair of orange-striped sawhorses blocking the area and a surly resident getting nasty with the uniformed officers for not letting him park in front of his apartment building. Good thing Gutierrez missed that turn or we would've still been struggling to get around that moron to flash our badges and get onto the scene.

Even though it wasn't my regular shift, I knew the men on duty, and thankfully they weren't weird around Psychs. I introduced Gutierrez and let the officer in charge walk us through the scene.

"The victim was found by his downstairs neighbor. Says she pounded on the ceiling with her broom handle so long that she put a hole through the plaster trying to get him to turn his music down. Came up to tell him to his face and found him…well, you can see for yourself."

"The door was unlocked," Gutierrez said, more than asked, and the officer nodded. She stopped at the door to slip on a pair of latex gloves and plastic booties. I looked at my jeans as I slipped the booties on over my holey Converse All-Stars and wondered if I'd gotten any jiz on them in Maurice's bathroom. I didn't bother with gloves since I didn't plan on touching anything.

Gutierrez paused in the victim's vestibule and then stepped aside to let me enter. She stared straight ahead of her into a living room where a couple of techs were setting down numbered cards around a sofa-bed and snapping photos. I came in behind her and nearly had to scoop my jaw up off the floor.

The victim was splayed buck naked on his red velvet bedspread like a piece of fucking performance art. Shards of mirror surrounded him, at first making it appear that a disco ball had taken vengeance on an unsuspecting naked guy. But on closer inspection, it was obvious that every piece had been painstakingly placed around the body so that, from the proper angle, the whole thing became a glittering, psychedelic swirl.

It might've even been fun to look at, given my current state of medication, if it weren't for the hot dead guy in the middle of it all. Not a mark on him, but obviously quite dead.

Gutierrez was already getting briefed. The victim was one Anthony Blakewood, twenty-seven, Caucasian, single, worked downtown in the Loop at a brokerage firm, no known enemies.

"Sexual penetration?" Gutierrez asked the Medical Examiner's tech, a thin girl with a blond ponytail who was still snapping photos.

"We haven't flipped the body yet, but it's a good possibility. The Coroner will have the final word on that."

I fixed my gaze on a completely irrelevant nail hole on the wall and pretended they weren't talking about anything gay. I always figure I'm going to get some kind of telltale look on my face and tip somebody off about my own "lifestyle." As far as I knew, the only one besides Hotshot Marks who might've guessed about me was Maurice, and Maurice just didn't talk about those kinds of things, period. That was that.

I then noticed that Blakewood had a little collection of miniature furniture with Scotty dogs painted on it, arranged on a semicircular shelf in the corner. Yeah. He was queer.

I wondered what I had in my apartment that would incriminate me to a casual observer. Not much, surprisingly. I tended not to hold onto stuff, because stuff usually held vibes, and vibes are a pain in the ass.

I almost ran my fingers through my hair again, but stopped myself just in time to keep from contaminating the crime scene by shedding. I jammed my hands into my pockets instead. The tech said that judging by the open container of lube nearby she'd just spotted, the victim had likely been penetrated, though the Coroner would have to verify that. A psycho murderer who lubed. How considerate.

Chapter 3

I stared up at my featureless white ceiling as I waited for the Seconal I'd taken to kick in. I'd loaned my car to Gutierrez with the stipulation that she wake me no earlier than noon. The victim hadn't spoken to me while I was at the apartment, and I'd taken three Auracels I needed to sleep off.

And while three was a pretty high dose for me, it wasn't like I'd never imbibed that many before. (Actually, my record is seven, but at that point you can't walk anymore and you tend to start vomiting.) Even after three Auracels, I should've been able to talk to Blakewood. Yeah, that's right. Even with my sixth sense trapped under all those meds, if I tried really hard, I should've been able to hear him. And I hadn't—not even a peep. So I was beginning to get concerned.

Anthony Blakewood, collector of Scotty dog miniatures, reamed out and discarded among several thousand other glittery bits. I wondered if he kind of dug it, being snuffed out in his prime and displayed so lovingly...or at least exactingly. I might have asked him as much, if I'd been able to find his ghost.

I dreamt of shards of silvered glass, seven years' bad luck and who's the fairest one of all. I woke with a post-Auracel sandpaper tongue and a piercing pain behind my right eye. I considered downing a handful of aspirin, but knew I'd only be asking for heartburn after lunch if I did.

I was at work on my second pot of coffee when Gutierrez called on the intercom. I buzzed her up from the lobby.

"Coffee?" I asked her as she stared over my shoulder and into my three-room apartment.

She hesitated for just a second, and then came in and took one of the two barstools by the kitchen counter. "Sure."

I looked around, not seeing the place anew, exactly, but reminding myself how stark it looks to a anyone who's never been there. "I'm kind of a minimalist."

Gutierrez' shoulders relaxed a little at my admission. "Is everything in here white?"

I handed her a white coffee mug and then pointed out the cream. She shook her head and sipped it black.

"White matches white," I said, and fiddled with my own cup, which had chilled and grown a skin on its surface. "I guess it seems easiest."

"I talked to the Coroner," she told me as I dumped my congealed coffee down the drain. "Our perp's even sicker than we thought."

You have absolutely no idea what I was thinking, I said to myself. But I didn't know her well enough to tease her like that. And besides, I didn't need anyone trying to read between the lines about anything I had to say on this particular case. With the gay and all. "Yeah?"

"The Coroner found pieces of mirror stuck under the victim's eyelids. But they'd been placed there so carefully they hadn't even scratched him."

I tried to imagine why I hadn't noticed that my victim had something angular beneath his closed eyelids, but since I was pretty much looking everywhere *but* at him, I wasn't very surprised. "I was so busy trying to talk to him..." I said, thinking that it wasn't altogether untruthful. I had tried.

"On Auracel?" Gutierrez asked. She drained her cup and came over to put it in the sink. "Why even bother?"

"I dunno." I pulled a black sportcoat off the peg on the back of my kitchen door. "I had to do something."

"We'll go try again now. You, uh.... You have better reception at the scene or at the morgue?"

Reception. I liked the way she was trying to

be so casual about it. "His spirit's probably at the apartment," I said. "Accidents, suicides and murders tend to be sticky."

"Okay, we'll start there." She offered me the keys, but I waved them toward her. She'd get to know the city that much quicker if she was the one who drove. And there was that lancing pain behind my eye to consider.

Traditionally, the younger partner was the one to do the driving anyway. Maurice let me slide on that responsibility when I told him that on bad days I tended to get visuals of accident victims, and that on certain intersections they got pretty numerous. They didn't look quite as solid as real pedestrians, but when you're doing forty-five on a residential street you don't necessarily have tons of time to study them. Maurice had said it explained a lot of the swerving I did. I'd let him think that. It seemed less incriminating than admitting that the Auracel didn't help my driving any, either.

At the scene I donned the plastic booties, and this time, the gloves, too. It irked me that the night before I'd been in the same room as a homicide victim and he hadn't said a word. But I was fairly clean now, having taken my last Auracel about twenty hours prior. I was ready to hear Blakewood's side of the story.

A couple of guys from the lab were combing through the apartment with their powders and brushes and ultraviolet wands. One of them muttered "Spook Squad" in a voice so low I almost didn't catch it, and the other one straightened his tie and looked nervous.

"Just tell me where we won't be in your way," I said. I was actually only paying them partial attention, because I was sure that any minute I'd be bowled over by Blakewood's spirit.

"Can you work from the kitchen?" the tech who'd called us Spook Squad asked. "We're done processing the kitchen."

I figured he wanted to get rid of us so they could gossip, and I almost suggested that Gutierrez and I go have a sandwich and come back later, when it occurred to me that a dead queer might very well be hanging out near the fridge. I jerked my head toward the kitchen doorway and Gutierrez followed me. Undoubtedly she'd been given a job description the size of the phone book, but I thought I could summarize for her in a few sentences.

"So here's how it works," I told her. "You record all the factual stuff, plus whatever impressions I give you. Then you record your impressions about my impressions." I peeked into the kitchen, but didn't see Blakewood in there. I was glad. I really didn't want a visual on those mirror eyes. "You score points for being as skeptical as humanly possible."

"So I'm supposed to shoot you down," she said.

I stepped into the kitchen and opened the fridge. Chinese takeout, Diet 7-Up and fat-free yogurt. "If my impressions are right, the facts'll back them up and you won't be able to debunk me."

"That's bullshit," she muttered. "We're partners. We've gotta watch each other's backs, not tear each other down."

"Hey." I gave her a smile over my shoulder. "Don't take it so personally. I never do." I liked hearing her swear. It left me free to do the same.

I walked into the kitchen and waited for that telltale sensation, like a drop in temperature that only I could feel, before the voices started. Except the kitchen was toasty, and the only sound in it was the motor on the refrigerator.

"Blakewood," I whispered, but the kitchen felt as flat and spiritless as...mine. "What's his first name?" I asked Gutierrez.

She flipped open her pad. "Anthony."

"Anthony," I said, figuring that maybe he'd died so horribly that he couldn't leave the side of his sofa bed. "Tony," I called softly. "You here?"

I planted my hands on my hips and looked around. Nothing.

Gutierrez stared at me with her pen poised over the tablet. She was a lefty. "Forget it," I said, easing past her into the small foyer. "There's nothing here."

I stood there while Gutierrez scratched what sounded like lots and lots of notes onto her pad. I didn't see the victim, didn't hear him. I wondered if it was possible that he died of natural causes and was just set up pretty by some kind of necrophiliac. Sure, that would be weird. But I've seen plenty of weird in my time.

"What now?" Gutierrez asked.

I crept closer to the archway that opened into the main room where we'd found him. "Anthony," I said, quiet, just barely moving my lips, but the tech who thought I was creepy blanched and started tugging at the collar of his shirt.

I listened hard, but didn't hear anything but the sound of Gutierrez' pen. "You're not picking anything up," she murmured, "are you?"

I shook my head just a tiny bit and we backed up into the vestibule. "We can come back when those guys are through," she offered. "Maybe they're blocking it."

I looked at a set of keys hanging beside the door. There was an embossed Scotty on the key fob. "Believe me, it'd take a lot more than a couple of guys with powderpuffs to block a fresh murder victim."

Gutierrez scratched out some more notes. "Okay, then. What if he didn't die here?"

I considered her theory. No one had

mentioned any evidence of the body being relocated, but given what I wasn't hearing, it made sense. Her brow furrowed, as if she'd found a hole in her own logic, but I thought we should explore the idea more conclusively before we shot it down.

"What if," I said thoughtfully.

Chapter 4

My cell phone rang, displaying the number for the Coroner's office. "The crime scene was definitely the victim's apartment."

Unfortunately, Gutierrez and I had come to the same conclusion, given that a neighbor had sworn he saw Tony walking back home that night with some new boyfriend he didn't recognize and, predictably, couldn't describe—except to say he was very handsome.

I sat in the passenger seat of my car and picked the brim of a styrofoam coffee cup into a dozen small, ragged pieces. I hesitated before letting them fall to the floor, and then I realized that it was my own damn car and I could do what I wanted. Styrofoam fluttered to the carpet around my shoes.

"That ever happen to you?" Gutierrez asked. "A dead guy that won't talk?"

"Never." I said it quietly, through clenched teeth, to keep myself from yelling at her. What did she know? It was her first time on the

Spook Squad...er, PsyCop Unit.

She flipped open her notepad, rested it against the steering wheel and scanned it. "There's gotta be a reason, then. Something unique to this case. We just need to figure out what it is."

My cell phone rang. I pulled it from my coat pocket and flipped it open. "Bayne."

"Gutierrez with you?" Warwick asked.

I refrained from asking him where the fuck else he thought my partner would be in the midst of an investigation. "Yeah."

"Get back to the station. Both of you." He hung up on me before I could try to figure out if he knew that the victim was giving me the silent treatment. What if one of the techs had overheard me talking to Gutierrez and had called him to tell him that I was a waste of taxpayer dollars? No, that was stupid. They had no idea how easy talking to dead victims usually was for me. They didn't know the silence was freaking me out.

If Gutierrez had any smarmy platitudes to offer on the way back to the squad house, she kept them to herself. The GPS unit beeped every now and then and styrofoam squeaked under my heels, but at least my performance anxiety wasn't exacerbated by a bunch of meaningless comforting phrases.

We went straight to Warwick's office. He

motioned for me to shut the door behind us. "Interesting report came through from Albuquerque today," he said.

Albuquerque? Gutierrez was from Albuquerque. I thought that was a pretty odd coincidence until I realized the whole face-to-face could very well be about her, and not me.

"Test results," he said, spreading the pages of a gray, degraded fax in front of us. "Did you know that your scores were identical on every psy-test you took, Lisa? Different tests, different days, and on each and every one you hit the exact score of random probability. To the percent?"

"Correct me if I'm wrong," I said, "but isn't that a good thing for a Stiff?"

"Stiffs vary," Warwick said, and I noted that a red flush had broken out across his formidable neck. "Usually between six and thirteen percent. This," he said, gesturing at the fax, "this is not random."

Gutierrez had ability? That probably explained what I'd seen in her right away that set me at ease. Normally I'd be happy to hear it, if she were my dry cleaner or my bridge partner. But certifiable psychics weren't allowed on the force without spending half a year training at Camp Hell. Otherwise known as Heliotrope Station, to those who've never done time there.

"You're off the case," Warwick said. "In fact,

you're off active duty until I can figure out what to do with you."

Gutierrez' face was a bland mask as she handed over her badge and gun. She hadn't said anything to defend herself. And she hadn't denied her ability, either. She turned and walked out without a word.

"Where are you with this case?" Warwick said to me. His voice seemed normal, but his color was way too high.

"We, um." I missed Gutierrez already. "The victim." I shrugged. "It's a tough one."

"I'll assign a pair of uniformed cops to back you up. Broaden your contact area and see what you can find."

Great. I'd have a pair of superstitious flat-foots following me around as I went from the cemetery to the victim's childhood home to anywhere else he liked to hang out while he'd been alive. I wondered if he had a favorite bar and, if so, the chances of eluding my babysit-ters and getting lucky. Ideally with Detective Marks, who'd just so happen to be there. Not that he hung out in gay bars or anything. At least, that's what I assumed, though I didn't hang out in gay bars either, so I didn't actually know for sure.

Warwick turned back to his notes and picked up the phone. I was dismissed.He'd call me when he had someone lined up. I could go to my desk and start trying to make sense in writing of what was going on, but writing had never been my strong point. Even Maurice, with his two-fingered, misspelled typing, was Shakespeare next to me.

I went out to my car with the intention of grabbing a very late lunch when I saw there was someone sitting in my drivers' seat. Since Gutierrez still had my keys, I realized that was a good thing.

"Wow," I said as I got in. "That was...." The fact that she'd been crying stopped me dead in my tracks. I can't stand it when girls cry.

"It's not fair," she said. "I earned this job."

I tried to recall a time in my life where I would've gotten as worked up as she was over a job, and failed. But that's just me. And then I had to remind myself that she'd needed to beat out a thousand other applicants to get it, and I could empathize at least a little.

"For what it's worth, I like working with you."

She gave me a sidelong glance. Her eyes, nose and lips were all red and puffy.

"What if I want to be a Stiff?" she said. "I make a better Stiff than a psychic. I'm a good cop. Really good."

"You got pretty far without being found out," I said. "Give yourself some credit for that." I realized that was a pretty stupid thing to say, since now that she'd been discovered, her career with the force was likely over.

She just hunched and looked down, getting tears on my steering wheel.

"Maybe they'd pay to retrain you. Your abilities might be bigger than you know."

"You saying I should try for Camp Hell?"

Oh. I wouldn't have wanted to be a woman there. It was hard enough being myself there.

"Look," I said, desperately trying to change the subject. "We shouldn't be sitting here like this in front of the station. Let's go to Dairy Queen. I'll buy you a milkshake."

"That's okay," she said. "You're gonna get called back in any time now. I'll just go home and try to figure out what I'm doing next." She pulled away from the curb into the lazy, midday traffic.

"Too bad I'm not precognizant," I said. "I'd try to give you some advice."

She smiled at that just a little, her eyes fixed on the road. "Your dead people got any ideas for me?"

I looked out over Montrose. "There's this fat Korean guy, hit by a bus, who's always hanging around the intersection at Damen. But I dunno that you want to follow his advice."

Gutierrez had picked a place in an old brick hotel less than a mile from the station. It'd been converted into studio apartments thirty years prior. The old lettering had been taken down long ago, but they'd left behind pale impressions on the brick that still read "Parker Inn."

My phone rang just as we got out of the car. She tossed me the keys over the hood and I had to juggle a little to grab them while I tried to flip my phone open. "Bayne."

"Get back to the station."

"Okay...?"

"There's been another murder."

Chapter 5

The vinyl miniblinds on Warwirck's door were tilted open and I could see him at his desk with his fingers steepled in front of his face as I approached. I opened his door and staggered back to avoid plowing into Jacob Marks, who'd been lurking to one side of the doorframe. I noted belatedly that his partner, Carolyn, sat on the other side of Warwick's desk with her hands folded on her lap. She was a neat, small blonde and her skirt suit fit a lot better than Gutierrez'.

"Got a call from the Police Commissioner," said Warwick, "and it seems we're gonna try something a little different." He said the word "different" like some people say "colored," or "alternative lifestyle."

"Detective Marks," Jacob said, sticking out his hand to shake mine. I took his hand in a daze and let him jerk my arm up and down. It was smart of him to pretend he didn't know me, I realized. And I supposed I looked blank enough to pull off his little act. "This is my partner, Carolyn Brinkman." Carolyn nodded. I stammered my name, wondering if she would notice that, technically, Jacob was lying to her. But maybe he wasn't. After all, her name was Carolyn Brinkman.

Warwick piped up. "Now I know that all of your training—years of training—says that a Psych and a Stiff are like salt and pepper, yin and yang, or whatever metaphysical bullshit you want to call it."

Ham and eggs, my brain said. Ernie and Bert. Shit and shinola. My brain could just go on and on for days. Apparently, it was panicking. Not enough to miss the fact that Marks looked like some kind of Italian supermodel in his suit. But enough to spew out random words that I had to struggle to keep from saying aloud.

"But the Commissioner don't give a damn what all your gurus and your mental masters say about the PsyCop pairbond. See, he don't work with PsyCops, not directly. He's old school. And if it were up to him, crimes would get solved with sweat and brains and elbow grease and luck."

"And maybe a few hundred thousand dollars' worth of the latest crime database technology," Marks added smoothly.

Warwick made a little barking sound, and I realized that it was a laugh.

I'd never made him laugh.

"But the Commissioner says we gotta do something," said Warwick, "and unless it puts one of my men at risk, we do it."

I looked at Carolyn with her hands folded on her knee, and at Marks, who may or may not have had a secret smile playing over his expression.

"He wants us to team up?" I asked. I'd almost used the analogy of a three-way, but considering that I'd had a literal petting session with Marks, I thought better of it.

"Exactly."

Marks pulled a leatherbound notepad from his inside pocket and flipped it open. "The case does straddle both of our jurisdictions."

"The second victim...?" I asked.

"Anal penetration and mirrors," said Warwick. "Happened two nights prior to Blakewood, according to the techs. You'll need to work out some kind of game plan to work the scene without stepping on each others' toes."

"Shouldn't be a problem," said Marks. "Carolyn and I would interview the victims ourselves, but our victims are usually alive. Seems natural for Detective Bayne to assume that duty. We'll handle the witnesses."

Warwick scribbled an address on a sticky note and handed it to me. The homicide was indeed on the border of the Twelfth and Fifth

Precincts. It was as if the perp had specifically chosen the very method and location that would bring Marks and me back together in a sea of fumbling awkwardness.

"I'll meet you there," I said quickly, and snatched the note from Warwick's hand. I'd rather fly solo than ride along with Marks in the back seat of his car like a third wheel while prim little Carolyn sat up front and continually adjusted the air conditioning.

I arrived to see Marks parallel parking his Crown Victoria with stunning accuracy in a space adjacent to the scene. I found a spot a block away in front of a hydrant, slapped my police permit atop my dashboard and started jogging toward the duplex.

And since when did I ever walk any more quickly than was absolutely necessary? I slowed my pace as I felt the prickle of sweat in my armpits.

Marks was talking to the uniformed officers on the scene. Carolyn turned to face me. "Sergeant Warwick wasn't very clear about what happened to your new partner."

My initial impulse was to make something up about Gutierrez, help her save a little face. And then I remembered that I was talking to the human polygraph. "Turns out she has some ability."

"That's too bad. It would be better to keep

our numbers even." She tugged her impeccable suit jacket down, though it hadn't needed straightening. "Next thing you know they'll be giving Psychs double duty, trying to spread us over two or three NPs." I hadn't heard that old term for Stiffs—NPs, or Non-Psychics—in ages. I guess it was more respectful, but still. I had to quell a smirk.

"But our ratio's tipped the other way," I pointed out. "Two Psychs to a Stiff."

"The brass won't look at it that way," she said. "Wait and see."

The thought of being told to do more work didn't worry me much. Overtime was fine by me. And when I felt overwhelmed, I'd just stand around and zone out, and everyone would assume I was talking to dead people. I think Maurice'd had his own way of doing the same thing. Sometimes I found pages and pages from his notepads covered in loop-de-loops.

Marks turned toward us and gave a little come-hither nod. I let Carolyn go first with the intention of tagging along behind the two of them, but Marks hung back so that he and I were side by side. "Sink or swim," he said.

"Desperate times call for desperate measures," I said, trading a maxim for a maxim.

Marks stopped in front of the victim's outer door and faced me. "Do you need anything from me in there that I should know about?

With Carolyn," he said, gesturing toward her, "I'm the muscle. The people we're interviewing don't get inside her personal space unless she wants them to. But you?" He shrugged, and his crisp suit rode up and down on his broad shoulders. "I don't know what you need."

I needed Maurice, was what I needed. I struggled to articulate what, exactly, he'd done for me. He was solid. He didn't judge me. He believed me.

Maybe that was really it. He believed that when I mumbled to myself, someone replied, and that when I stared really hard, there was something there, even if he couldn't see it himself.

"General backup is fine," I said.

Marks gave me a withering look. I wasn't trying to be cagey. It just came out that way.

Ryan Carson was a junior architect at a high-priced firm that dealt with gigantic corporate clients. His duplex was probably worth a cool half-mil, and the interior looked like a great big Ikea display. Queer.

I snapped on the plastic booties and edged into the master bedroom, mouth-breathing against the smell. The closet had once had mirrored doors, but what remained of them was scattered around the room. I squinted and saw that the shards were set in more of a burst pattern than a swirl this time around, as if the killer couldn't stand to repeat himself exactly.

Ryan Carson was splayed in the middle, arms and legs outstretched like he was in the midst of winning some Olympic event, naked and triumphant, though starting to bloat in the middle. His eyelids looked wrong. Covering bits of mirror, I guessed.

But where was Ryan Carson's spirit? I looked around the room and saw nothing but a pair of techs, one snapping photographs and the other taking notes. "Ryan?" I said, quiet, but the techs heard. I'd worked scenes with each of them dozens of times before, but there was still that little pause while they seemed to steel themselves against my presence.

And to make matters worse, Ryan wasn't talking.

I usually got visuals on murders. The spirits were just so pissed off, they couldn't wait to tattle on whoever'd done it. Cases where the victim knew the perp were practically open and shut. But there was no visual on Ryan. Or anything else, for that matter. Just a cold dead body on a bed surrounded by mirror fragments.

I headed to Ryan's kitchen just in case he was hanging out there. On the way, I passed Carolyn and Marks. Carolyn was grilling a witness in a quiet and professional manner, while Marks loomed behind her, looking very big and threatening while he took notes. I had to give it to them, they certainly did have their method down pat.

The kitchen, a landscape of black enamel and stainless steel, was empty.

I cycled through the various rooms, edging around the perimeter and doing my best to fly under everyone else's radars. The Auracel was ancient history by then, and I should have picked up Ryan about as easily as I could order a pizza. So where was he?

I strained so hard in the living room that I actually got a visual on a dead goldfish. He just floated there above the mantle, looking translucent and bored. If Ryan's spirit was around, it wasn't in the living room.

The duplex had an attic—not the finished kind where there's a guest room and a spot for out-of-season clothes, but the creepy kind where you've got to pull a set of folding stairs out of the ceiling to get up there. I'd had no luck anywhere else, so I decided to see if maybe Ryan was haunting the attic.

The feeling up there was calm, though through the vents I could hear people on the street chattering, and the squeak of investigators' feet treading up and down between the first and second floors drifted up through the trap door. Ryan had a lot of stuff up there, but it was all boxed and labeled. Christmas decorations, camping gear, a bunch of old board games.

I reached out to him with my mind, trying to composite the dead body on the bed with the snapshots stuck to the fridge and come up with a semblance of how the victim had really looked. "Don't you want us to get this sonofabitch?" I asked aloud. "C'mon, Ryan. Throw me a bone."

I listened, and I reached. Nothing. I walked farther in, crouching beneath the slope of the roofline and squinting to make out the blocky architect's writing on the boxes: College. Badminton set. Mom's House. As my gloved fingers brushed against the final crate, I thought I heard the distant sound of a woman crying. But it was gone so quickly I couldn't have said for sure.

Chapter 6

We reconvened back at the Twelfth Precinct, since Carolyn and Marks were the only two with tangible work to show for our afternoon of digging. Neither of them seemed to think it was unusual that I hadn't gotten a hit from the crime scene. And I don't think either of them would've hesitated to question me if they had. They were both similar shades of blunt, though Carolyn tended to be so soft-spoken she almost came off as polite.

"So the guy from the newsstand saw Ryan the architect come home with a Chinese guy," said Marks, "and the cab driver swears the second man was Pakistani. Is that what I'm hearing?"

Carolyn's gaze went wide, like she was watching a movie screen inside her head. "They were positive, Jacob. Absolutely certain."

"But given the timeframe," said Marks, "about twelve thirty p.m., they had to be talking about the same guy."

I broke in. "Maybe he was just, uh...tanned."

I felt like an idiot the second I opened my mouth, but Carolyn's answer took the sting off.

"I thought of that," she said. "But when I was reading the witnesses, it wasn't a skin tone they'd noticed. From the guy at the newsstand, I kept getting images of his cousin back home. And the cab driver thought the subject looked exactly like some Eastern movie star."

"Then something else is going on," Marks suggested. "The perp's got talent and he's doing something to obscure his identity."

"We don't have enough to go on to work that theory," Carolyn said.

"Not yet," said Marks. "We'll have to dig up some more witnesses."

He looked at me. I wondered if he wanted me to find some dead people at the scenes, other than the victims, to canvas. How could I tell him that they'd both been total paranormal voids—except for the goldfish?

I hoped he could make do with a little show of support. "It's worth looking into," I said.

Carolyn flipped through Marks' notes and made ticks by a couple of his observations. "It's all we've got," she said, "so we might as well try."

We hit the street again and broadened our net. Anthony Blakewood, the Scotty collector, had likely picked up his date at a gay nightclub on Belmont that wouldn't open for another four hours. We did trace Ryan Carson's path back to a coffee house on Clark, though.

I was parking-challenged yet again and found Carolyn and Marks already there, questioning a barista. The girl was college-aged and chunky, and intent on battering a piece of chewing gum into submission with her molars. Carolyn made little squiggles and ticks on Marks' notepad while they talked.

"I'm sure you see hundreds of people every day," Marks was saying, "but just think back and see if this man is familiar."

I flashed my badge and mumbled my name as I fell into place beside Carolyn. The employee gave me the briefest once-over and then focused on Marks' photo of Ryan.

"Oh, I dunno. Working in Boystown, they all start looking the same. Especially these quiet, plain ones."

I don't know that I would have called Ryan plain. He'd had a nice build and a sincere, open look about him. But maybe she meant plain compared to the kids with pierced eyebrows, noses and lips talking computer games over their lattes.

"Three nights ago," Carolyn prompted. "Maybe he lingered a while."

The barista began to shake her head, but then went still. "Oh yeah. The chai. That's right." She pointed toward the window. "He was sitting up there with a Powerbook and he had a croissant special, no meat."

"Them fucking fags. Maybe they'd get straightened out if they ate a little meat like regular people."

I swung around but there was no one visible behind me. The gargly, decayed quality of the voice clicked in my head and I felt my mind shift to a different kind of listening. I recalled the idea I'd had earlier about interviewing a dead witness. Whatever I learned wouldn't be admissible in court since technically it would be hearsay, but I was open to anything that'd help narrow down our search.

I reached over Marks' shoulder for the photo of Ryan and tried to pretend that I didn't notice the barista looking at me funny. "Could I, um...? Thanks."

I turned away from Marks and held the photo in front of my chest. "Did you see this man Friday night?" I spoke so softly that your average NP would think I was talking to myself.

"That one? Yeah. He comes in here two, three times a week and has a *chai.*"

"Mmm hm. And was he with anybody?"

Gooseflesh rose on my arms as whomever I was speaking to grew excited. "How could I forget? Some faggot wearing a Halloween costume in June."

"Oh," I said, disappointed. "Like a drag queen? A transvestite?"

"You know I had a clean bill of health not three months before I kicked the bucket? Then they cracked me open. Massive coronary, they said. Arteries seventy-eight percent blocked. It's them HMOs that's the problem, ya know. Turn people around like short order cooks."

"What was she dressed as? The female impersonator."

"Are you stupid? When'd I say there was a Cher with a pecker in here, huh? That's nothing new. Them faggots do that all year 'round. I'm talking a real costume."

I imagined a mascot gone astray—maybe someone dressed as a hot dog. "Describe it," I said. I'd raised my voice a little, but Marks and Carolyn had shifted their bodies to block anyone from disturbing me. Their postures were casual, but their timing was fantastic.

"Scary," said the disembodied voice. "I dunno. Lots of black, like a big cape with a hood."

"What was he, a white guy? Hispanic? Young, old?"

"I...I dunno." The voice wavered and grew softer. "I couldn't see his face."

"How to you know it was a man?"

"I dunno. I just do."

A shiver coursed through me and my relative temperature returned to normal. I guess the dead blowhard couldn't stand being asked a question that he couldn't answer with obnoxious certainty.

I turned back to Marks and Carolyn, who were both staring at me, anticipation glittering in their eyes.

"The man who ordered the chai," I asked quietly. "Was he with somebody in a cloak?"

The barista burst out laughing. "What, like Dracula?"

I felt my cheeks color. "Maybe something *like* a cloak. A rain poncho. A long duster."

"I think I'd remember someone in a cloak," she snickered, then turned her attention back to Jacob Marks.

Chapter 7

I made a mental note to reintroduce myself to the bar scene. Even if I'd had a drink or two in me, the music was so loud that I probably wouldn't be bothered by disembodied sob stories. Unfortunately, no live person at the bar knew Anthony Blakewood well enough to have any idea who he'd gone home with. Any dead bar-hoppers were drowned out by the music, and no one even cruised me. So the trip to the GloryWhole was a total bust.

I split off from Carolyn and Marks around 11:30 and swung by a 7-11 for something to eat. I reached for an avocado wrap, but then I remembered what the dead creep at the coffee house had said about queers and vegetarians, and opted for a roast beef instead. Halfway back to the counter I turned around and exchanged the beef for the avocado again. And I did my best to ignore the mostly-transparent guy with the afro jacking off in the corner, and the voice coming from aisle three that kept repeating, "But he loves me. I can't leave him."

I ate as I drove home, wondering how it was that I was queer enough to pick out an avocado wrap, but not queer enough to get cruised at a gay bar. It could've been my badge that they were avoiding, sure. But I think the idea of laying a cop gets a lot of guys off. And besides, plenty of 'em were drooling over Marks, not that I blame them. I took a bite of the wrap and mayonnaise squirted out the end and dribbled down my lapel. I steered with my knee while I tried to wipe it off, but only succeeded in getting mayo all over my hand. Maybe it was my wardrobe that was the problem. Not that I had any intention of doing anything about it in the near future, since I think shopping's about as much fun as going to the dentist.

I finished the wrap before I got home and spent an extra minute trying to get mayo off my sportcoat. I gave up when it became obvious that all I'd accomplished was embedding rolled-up fragments of cheap paper napkin all over myself. I realized that I'd dropped my other coat off at the dry cleaner's about four months prior. And I wondered if they would give the thing to me without the pickup slip, or if they'd foisted it off on Goodwill by now.

To top things off, the ghost of Jackie the Loudmouthed Prostitute had ranged up from her normal turf about two blocks south to tell me, yet again, about the john who'd shanked her. If I'd known about Jackie, I might have picked a different apartment. But she hadn't made her first nocturnal appearance until I'd completed my week long stake-out and written a check for the security deposit. Sometimes I thought about moving, but I reminded myself that she only harassed me a couple of times a month. The spirits around my old place had managed to waylay me every single week.

"So I said, 'You got a place, baby?' And he said, 'Come on over here, sugar, no one can see us back in this here alley.'"

Though they were infrequent, her tirades tended to get on my very last nerve. "Go find someone who gives a shit," I said, pushing open the gate to my walkway.

"Are you disrespecting me?" I felt a small chill, like Jackie might be gearing up for a temper tantrum, but it was weak enough that I was able to blow it off. "You hear me, white boy? I said, are you disrespecting me?"

There's a technique Camp Hell taught people like me—spirit mediums, to use the technical term—for when we were done talking. We're supposed to surround the entity with a bubble of light, white on the inside to draw them toward the light, and blue on the outside, to protect us from any potential malevolence. I thought real hard about putting one of those bubbles around Jackie. I formed it in my mind and I pushed until my ears popped, imagining my power coursing out to surround her and get her the fuck away from me.

But that was apparently all in my head.

"No one talks to Jackie that way," her voice continued. "You know what I'm sayin'? White boy—do you know what I'm sayin'?"

"Talk to the hand," I said, and waved her off as I went into my vestibule. She'd never yet followed me into the building. I think it might've been too far away from the spot where she'd died. At least, I hoped it was.

About a foot of free newspapers and sales fliers were piled up on the floor. They'd drifted back against the security door, preventing it from shutting completely. One of these days I was going to fling all that crap out onto the lawn. But not while I was covered in mayonnaise and had a pissed off hooker ghost railing at me from the courtyard.

I stuck my mail key into the bank of mailboxes on the wall, wiggled it to get it to that precise depth where it would turn, and opened my mailbox. Sales fliers slipped out and I let them join the rest of the paper on the floor. I studied what was left. A phone bill. A free sample of shampoo and conditioner all in one.

The outer door swung open, startling me,

and I half-turned as a bulky figure pressed me into the open mailbox. "You know how hot you look when you talk to yourself in coffee shops?" Marks said. The cellophane-wrapped plastic packet of shampoo crinkled between us while he leaned in for a kiss. The after-work stubble around his goatee scraped my cheek, and he tasted like cinnamon gum.

I pulled back from the kiss, though, wanting to make sure that I had things straight. "You're not pissed off that you got stuck with me for this case?"

Marks tilted his head. His features were harsh in the yellow buglight. "I've got two Psychs on my team. Why should I be pissed?" He leaned forward again and his lips were softer on mine, gently caressing my mouth and parting my lips for a slow, tender sweep of his tongue. My knees went all rubbery.

Evidently, he wasn't worried about us getting caught fraternizing—and if he wasn't concerned, then I sure wasn't gonna make a stink. I'd always thought that rules were just for people who tended to get caught.

"Look," I said when he let me come up for air. I was just about to tell him that I could hear Jackie screaming about her no-good pimp and it was a total buzzkill, but I decided it would be better to take the paranormal things slowly since my talents were probably much freakier than Carolyn's. "Let's go upstairs."

We sprinted up to the third floor like we hadn't just spent ten hours combing for witnesses. I had my key in my hand, poised at lock-level, when I rounded the top of my stairs and saw that some long-haired woman was slumped against my front door. I was fairly sure she was alive, too.

The girl sniffled. Marks stopped behind me on the second stair to the top. I stared at her and tried to place her, and then recognized the oxford-blue blouse that had once been hidden by an ill-fitting suitcoat. "Gutierrez?" I said.

She peered at me through the zig-zag waves of her unbraided hair.

I tried to act like it wasn't all that unusual to find someone sprawled at my front door. "Marks, this is my partner, Lisa Gutierrez."

Marks stepped up beside me and peered down at her. Gutierrez made no move to stand. She seemed kind of distant. I wondered if she'd been drinking. Or maybe if she'd slit her wrists and I just couldn't see the puddle of blood due the lousy hall lighting.

She squinted at me and then nodded, as if she'd only just placed me. "Good, you're here. Ask me a question."

"Huh?"

"Just ask me," she said. She seemed to have a Spanish accent that I hadn't noticed before.

"Something with a yes or no answer."

I shook my head. "What, trivia?"

"Anything," she said, drawing the word long and pronouncing the end like "theeng."

"Am I married?" Marks asked.

Gutierrez swung her head around to peer at him. Her brow furrowed. I waited for steam to come out of her ears. "I don' know. Ask something else."

Marks glanced at me and raised his eyebrow. I shrugged. "Am I Jewish?" he said.

Gutierrez thought hard, and then nodded with a satisfied smile. "I don' know."

Marks pulled a pen light out of his suit-coat, crouched down in front of Gutierrez and shined the beam in her face. "She's the one with the gift they just discovered, right?"

I nodded.

Gutierrez just sat there while Marks looked her over. "You give her any of your Auracel?"

"What, are you crazy? That's way too strong for someone without any tolerance." And then I took in her wooziness and her general ennui and I had to wonder. Where would she get ahold of something so tightly controlled— something for which I just happened to have a prescription? And then I remembered. The pill in my glove box.

Good thing it was only a halfsie or we'd probably be on our way to the emergency room.

I reached over Gutierrez' head to unlock my front door with the goal of getting Gutierrez inside and getting rid of Marks. "I can...uh... take it from here," I said.

Marks looked at me like I was nuts. "What, you just remembered you're not single or something? I thought you invited me up two minutes ago." He'd started helping Gutierrez to her feet as if caring for a massively stoned partner was all in a day's work.

"I hadn't planned on...." I gestured toward Lisa.

Marks managed to support Gutierrez with one arm and reach over me to push open my front door with the other. "But you know what to do, right? There's some kind of hangover cure for anti-psyactives, isn't there?"

"No," I said, mostly to myself. "Not really."

I hurried inside before them to flip on the light and made sure there wasn't a kitchen stool in the middle of the floor waiting for someone to trip over it. Marks looked around as he pulled Lisa inside. "Postmodern Institutional. Nice."

I bristled at the "institutional" remark, and did my best not to have a Camp Hell flashback. I supposed Marks thought he was being witty. Just because he was turning out to be a Psych groupie didn't mean that a psychic had ever told him a Heliotrope story. Most of us did our best to forget them.

"Put her on the futon," I said, figuring I could just buy another plain canvas cover if Lisa ended up puking on it. Marks steered her into the living room. I ran the tap until the water was as cold as it was going to get and then looked in the freezer for some ice. Both ice cube trays were empty. I wondered why I'd just left them there like that.

"Vic," Lisa said as she saw me come through the living room door. "You gotta do something for me." Marks sat beside her on the couch, relaxed, but keeping an eye on her.

I handed her the glass of water and some slopped onto her knee. "I'll try."

She leaned forward and more water dribbled onto the hardwood floor. "Tell my Papa I'm a good cop."

"I'm sure he thinks so," I said. "Parents are always proud when their kids make the force."

She shook her head, but the remainder of the water stayed in the glass. "Crackhead shot him down when I was seventeen. He don't know."

"He was a cop?" Marks asked.

Lisa nodded. "Twenty-three years."

I closed my eyes and tried to figure out how to sound genuine without being too truthful. Because chances were that Gutierrez' father was walking around in an outdated uniform complaining about the sonofabitch who'd shot him and reliving it down to the last freaking detail. Murders just are that way.

"They didn't have PsyCops then," Lisa said. "Not out west." She stared at me through her hair and it disturbed me, seeing her like that, her control stripped away by the drug. "He thought I wouldn't be nothing better than a fortune teller like my *abuelita*."

Marks was listening intently. He'd followed me home to have a good time, and he was getting it—just not in the form he'd expected. "What's your talent, Lisa?"

She clutched the water glass hard and turned her face toward him. "My sister and me call it *sí-no*."

"Sí-no."

"The yes-no game. We played it all the time. Will it rain tomorrow? Yes. Is Mama making chicken tonight? No. Will I like my new teacher? Yes."

"Limited precog," I said.

"Maybe not so limited," said Marks. "I'll bet she can work some pretty big questions into the *sí-no*."

"And her psych tests," I said. "That's how she managed to come out completely average. She knew that anything consistently above or below would have filtered her into the positive or negative psychic tiers, so she got half the questions right, half wrong, on purpose. Maybe you're right. Maybe her gift is incredibly accurate."

Marks eyed her greedily. "Can you imagine what she'd do with some training?"

I closed my eyes and remembered the night at Camp Hell when the doctors in surgical masks blew my synapses wide with a powerful psyactive. They'd left me strapped to a gurney for three days until I stopped twitching. "Training's a very personal thing," I said, doing my best to keep my voice even.

"My Papa'd want me to be a real cop."

I supposed I could've taken offense at the implication that I wasn't one, but maybe I secretly agreed with her. "Don't worry about that now," I said. "Get some sleep." I stood up to scrounge a blanket off my own bed while Marks managed to open out the futon with Lisa still on it.

Once we'd gotten her settled, Marks headed toward my bedroom. I followed him and paused in the doorway, watching him loosen his tie. "I don't think you should stay," I whispered.

"Why not?"

I glanced back toward the living room. "I'm not, um. Y'know."

"What?"

I crossed my arms and sighed, and hated

that he was going to make me say it. "Out."

He smirked. "Not to anyone? You don't strike me as a virgin."

"Don't be stupid. You're a cop, too."

Marks eased over to me a hell of a lot more gracefully than someone his size had the right to. "I don't show up at the squad house in a pink tutu, no. But my family? My friends? My partner? I'm not gonna waste my time and energy playing games with them."

I looked back at Lisa, wondering if she was asleep or just zoning out with her eyes shut. "I only met her a couple of days ago," I said in my own lame defense. That was my excuse for not telling my partner. Family and friends? That was simple. I didn't have any.

Marks pulled a business card from the breast pocket of his suitcoat and tucked it down the collar of my shirt. He pressed his lips against my ear and spoke softly, his voice a low buzz. "Call me on my cell if you need anything." His tongue traced the outline of my ear and then darted inside to draw a long shiver out of me. "Anything."

I stared at the kitchen doorway long after Marks was gone.

Chapter 8

I swabbed the shower out before Lisa woke up. Just because my whole apartment's white doesn't mean I'm a clean freak or anything, and I'd started noticing dust bunnies, clumps of hair, and fingerprints that would send a woman running for the Formula 409.

"I think my eyeball is gonna fall out."

I turned to find Lisa leaning against the doorframe of the tiny bathroom, picking a tangle out of her hair.

"Yeah. I get that, too." I turned on the hot tap and ran water into the tub. "A shower and a couple of aspirin will help. A little."

Lisa stared down at her nails. "I feel like I should ask you if I did anything stupid last night, except I actually remember it all."

I sat on the edge of the clawfoot tub and played with the white vinyl shower curtain that hung from an oval track suspended from the ceiling. I noticed some mildew on the bottom and tried to hide it in one of the folds.

"Who was that other detective? He your new partner?"

"Temporarily. He works for another precinct and he's already got a partner."

"That's too bad. He seemed like a good cop."

I found a black T-shirt in my closet that I'd accidentally bought a size too large and never worn, and tossed it into the bathroom while averting my eyes. Then I brewed some double-strong coffee and wondered if Lisa would have the stomach for chicken pot pies for breakfast. Probably not. We'd need to eat out.

Lisa emerged from the steamy bathroom with the end of a tight braid pinched between her fingers. My T-shirt was stretched taut on her, making her seem chestier than she'd looked in a suit. "Got a rubber band?"

"Um...doorknob."

Lisa found a band and wrapped it around the end of her braid.

"How's your power today?" I asked her.

"I dunno." She sat on the second stool and took the cup of black coffee I handed her. "I think it's coming back. Answers pop into my mind when I ask questions, but I don't feel so sure of them."

"It comes back gradually," I said. "We're people. You can't turn us on and off like TV sets."

Lisa sipped her coffee and winced. "You

really gotta clean out your coffee pot."

"Put some cream in there, you won't notice it so much." Lisa attempted to gag some coffee down while I slid a couple of aspirin her way. "If you want, I can take you somewhere with decent coffee."

Lisa peered at me suspiciously.

"Where the second murder victim just happened to be hanging out the night of his death," I added.

Lisa's eyes went wide. "You can't do that, Vic. You'll get in trouble bringing me in on the case while I'm suspended."

"But we're just going out for a little coffee," I protested.

Lisa looked into her cup. "The second crime scene—all covered with mirrors like the first one?"

I nodded.

"Those poor boys," she said, getting up to dump her coffee into the sink. That seemed like an odd thing to say, considering that they were probably about her age, but I didn't remark on it.

A kid with a pierced eyebrow was working the counter and I was relieved that I didn't have to deal with the gum-chewing girl who'd seen me talking with the dead guy. I got a latte and a chocolate chip bagel while Lisa just ordered a black coffee, extra tall. "Let's sit over here," I said, carrying our coffees to a table while balancing my bagel in the crook of my arm. I gestured toward a table in front with a tilt of my head. "That's where the second victim supposedly had chai with Darth Vader."

"And a dead witness told you this," said Lisa. She peeled off the lid and blew on her coffee. "Dead guys ever lie?"

"Why don't I ask you, Miss *si-no*. Do dead guys ever lie?"

Lisa grinned. "Yes."

"And they get their stories all mixed up, too," I told her. "They're just as thick as the living. Sometimes worse, since they get stuck in these crazy ruts and keep repeating themselves."

She wrinkled her nose. "You hear any dead people talking now?"

I shifted my focus but the room felt quiet. "Not now. But this is a new building. The older ones almost always have someone hanging around. It's worse at night."

"No wonder you take Auracel. Once I took that pill and the *si-no* was gone, I felt kinda lonely. I couldn't figure out why you'd want to get rid of your power—unless it stopped you from doing your job. But I guess it's pretty different from mine."

"And how could you ever think that a talent like *si-no* would stop you from doing yours? You put yourself in some hot water by applying to be a PsyCop. If you'd just stayed in the regular force, you'd probably make detective with the first opening. What were you thinking?"

Lisa slouched against the back of her chair. "The *si-no* told me to. I saw the job posted in the breakroom, with about a hundred others. PsyCops, they're still pretty novel in New Mexico. 'Should I apply for that job?' I asked myself. *Si*."

The *si-no* told me to. The courts would have a field day with that explanation.

My cell phone rang—Marks. "Carolyn and I are at the Twelfth putting our notes together, and it looks like at least three more witnesses who saw the suspect would identify him differently."

"Hold on," I said. I hit the mute button on my phone and turned to Lisa. "Did the same person murder both Blakewood and Carson?"

"Yes."

"And is he doing something to disguise his appearance?"

"No."

I un-muted my phone. "Something's definitely up with the killer," I said, "but I'll be damned if I know what it is."

"I think it warrants some serious discussion over dinner tonight. Say eight o'clock? Cottonwood Lounge."

I stared hard at my phone. The restaurant

was fancy enough that I could hardly mistake the invitation for anything but a date. And it was nowhere near either of our precincts. Marks was persistent, I'd give him that. "Um... okay. Sure."

"See you then," he purred, and the noise of his line cut off.

I realized Lisa was staring at me. "Ask me," she said.

"Huh?"

"You want to ask me a *sí-no*. I can tell."

I drummed my fingers on the faux-marble tabletop. "Is Marks..." I started, and then wondered how to phrase my question. The incriminating part seemed to be out of the bag with just that single word—his name. "Is he just some kind of player, messing with my head?"

"No." Lisa blushed a little and turned her attention toward the remainder of her coffee. I wondered if what I'd just done counted as "coming out" to my partner. Lisa was no dummy, so I suspected that was a "yes."

I dropped Lisa off at her apartment and went back to my desk at the Fifth, figuring I'd hunt-and-peck my way through what little I had to report while I counted down the minutes until eight p.m.

I'd been there a couple of hours when my

phone buzzed and Betty the receptionist's voice came through. "Detective Bayne?"

"Yeah?"

"Sergeant Warwick wants to see you."

Betty'd been at the station for something like forty years. She was the main reason they still used the same phone system they'd installed in the early eighties. But I gave her credit. She could take the most mundane sentence and, with the addition of a well-placed but subtle inflection, let you know exactly what was going on.

In this case, the way she lingered over the word "see" implied that I was in some kind of deep shit.

Warwick knew about me and Marks. That was all I could figure. I could see it now, a great big scandal. Two members of the already-controversial Paranormal Investigation Unit fired in a shocking gay sex scandal—details at eleven.

Warwick stood up and loomed over his desk as I came in. I closed the door behind me so fewer desk cops could hear me getting reamed. "You want to tell me what you were doing meeting with Gutierrez earlier today?" he demanded.

A small, giddy part of me wanted to tell him that I was fucking her. But then I thought of Marks, strong enough to tell his inner circle who he actually was, and I thought better of it. Besides, how could I do that to Lisa's reputation?

"We were discussing anti-psyactives," I told him, figuring that even Carolyn the lie detector wouldn't be able to find anything wrong with that explanation.

Warwick frowned, sure that I wasn't being truthful, but unable to discount what I'd said without challenging me. "You are not to discuss the case with her," he warned me. "She's suspended. And if I find out you're leaking evidence to her, that's where your ass is gonna be, too."

"Yes, sir." I suspect that legally he couldn't tell me not to see her on my own time. But it seemed that he thought if he glared at me hard enough, I would infer it.

Warwick picked up his phone and told Betty to get his wife on the line—his way of dismissing me without giving me the courtesy of saying it aloud. Maybe most NPs really think that every Psych is a mind reader, but Warwick was taking it that one extra step just to be an ass.

Chapter 9

I hoped that buying a new jacket at SaverPlus Department Store wouldn't mark me as a complete and utter loser for the rest of my life, but I'd ended up working until 6:45 and needed to get something fast. An ancient salesman who smelled like cigars kept yammering on about how I needed a 39 long, an unusual size, but he thought he might have it in navy. I grabbed a 40 regular in black and headed for the cashier while he was still rummaging around.

I pulled the tags off in the car while I cursed at the GPS for taking me through the most congested six-way intersection in the city. I popped open my glove box and searched for a comb each time the traffic lurched to a fitful stop. Not that I'd ever actually put a comb in there. But it seemed like it'd be a likely place to keep one.

When I got to the Cottonwood Lounge, I found Marks sitting at the tastefully set table, sipping a glass of dark red wine like he didn't even notice I was fifteen minutes late. "I, um... traffic was lousy."

He shook his head from side to side like I'd said something funny. "Wine?"

"Wine? Um, no." I pointed to my head. "Doesn't agree with me."

"Really?"

I sensed that he wanted me to give him some kind of Psych story to gnaw on, but I just wasn't up for it. "Warwick laid into me for having contact with Gutierrez."

I thought he would ask me how Warwick knew, but instead he just shrugged and drained his glass. "And you're so worried about what Warwick thinks."

"He is my boss."

"How many years?"

I counted back, just to be sure. "Twelve."

"You were in one of the original three PsyCop units when the whole thing was hardly more than a crazy experiment. Your hit rate was the only thing that kept the program alive, especially after that witchhunt exposé on the psychic gambling ring that Channel 2 aired. You think he doesn't remember that?"

I sipped my ice water and thought back. Those things had all happened. But I didn't recall anyone ever acting like they were anything special.

Marks leaned forward and his casual

demeanor fell away. Intensity blazed in his dark eyes, and he grasped my forearm from across the table. "We're gonna nail this bastard. Me and you. Carolyn and Lisa. And then see what kind of respect you command."

I considered Marks. It was easy enough for him to be confident. This case was like any other to him: get evidence, put evidence together, solve case. But me? My evidence collection was on the fritz and it was really starting to piss me off.

Over dinner I managed to get marinara sauce on my new blazer, though it left less of a telltale mark than the mayonnaise had on my old one. But at least I found Marks to be pretty good company—a lot easier to talk to than other men I'd attempted to date. There'd been the record store clerk who got squeamish when he found out I carried a gun. And the hairdresser who couldn't stop making wisecracks about my handcuffs. But Marks just commented on the food and gave me sultry looks between every bite he took. I could handle that.

I followed him back to his place, a small second-floor condo on the lake. It looked more lived-in than the architect's duplex, but just about as expensive. A phantom cat sat on his radiator, tail lashing back and forth, but other than that we were alone.

"It's good," I said, happy to get out of that new sportcoat. I threw it over the arm of his burgundy leather couch. "No one here but us."

Marks grinned as if he'd been waiting for me to say something spooky all night. He loosened his tie like he was doing a striptease, then pulled it off and let it fall in a silk heap on top of my jacket. I was relieved that he wasn't compulsively neat. "C'mere," he said. He put his arm around me, led me to a floor-to-ceiling window and pulled open a set of vertical blinds.

The lake spread out before us, tiny lights flashing here or there where a boat floated at anchor, and the yellow grids of high rise windows glowing in my peripheral vision. I'm not usually one to go out of my way to see the sights, but the view from Marks' window was pretty nice. "Wow."

His hands slipped around my middle as I said it, and my breath hitched as he pulled my shirt from my waistband. I felt his palms glide over my bare stomach and I shivered as he fit himself to the curve of my back, his breath warm on my neck.

I tried to turn around and face him, but he had me spread up against the plate glass window and there was no way I'd be able to move unless he let me. He pressed into me harder, grazing the nape of my neck with his teeth as his hands slid higher. His fingers closed over my nipples and he took them gently, just rolling them, rolling, rolling, as his teeth combed my neck and the bulge of his cock rubbed against the back of my pants.

I reached back over my shoulder with one hand to see if I could touch him, stroke him, anywhere. But I was splayed like a bug on the glass and couldn't do anything but writhe while Marks' hands played over my chest and his mouth seared tingling trails over my neck. Eventually I stopped trying and just pressed my cheek into the window, my breath fogging the lake skyline until it took on the spectral look of the dead world that dogged my existence.

Marks teased my nipples until they were stiff and then squeezed them harder—just a little—until I groaned aloud and pushed my ass back against him. He pressed his teeth into me and held me there by my neck while his hands slid downward and made short work of my fly. My slacks pooled around my ankles and my cock stood out in my boxer briefs, the tip butting against the cool glass through the thin fabric.

Once my pants were off, Marks' hands slid up my sides, along my ribs. They crossed themselves over my chest as he pressed himself into my back from chin to thigh. "Just stay there," he said, his voice low and rough. "I want to get you off."

Had he actually said that? Had anyone ever said that to me before? Ever? Another of my breaths bloomed against the window as Marks dropped to his knees behind me and took the waistband of my underwear between his teeth. My damp fingertips squeaked at the glass, searching for something to grasp, while Marks' goatee whispered across the skin of my bare ass as he tugged my underwear down. The briefs got caught over my hard-on, which was now sticking up at an angle, and he nibbled around the plane of my hip and the bony crest of my pelvis as he worked at undressing me. My cock snapped free and the glass was colder than I thought it would be, though maybe the smear of precome I was painting there was giving me a chill.

His head dipped low as he wedged it under my butt and pressed his lips against my inner thigh, trailing his hot tongue in slow swashes that inched higher and higher. My legs trembled as I stepped out of the underwear and spread my feet, the length of my cock now forced vertically between my belly and the glass that was no longer cold; the heat of my body had warmed it.

Marks' warm, damp breath enveloped the back of my balls as he sighed, and then his tongue was there, teasing at them as they shifted inside my scrotum, which wrinkled at the touch of his mouth. He kissed them and laved them and bathed them with his tongue, and all the while I jammed my cock against his window, squeaking it up, then down, and wishing there was something warm or wet or fleshy against it instead of a pane of hard, smooth glass.

"Please," I mumbled against the window while his tongue traced the divot between my balls.

"Please what?" he said, his mustache tickling me right below the asshole while his hot breath had me squirming.

Damn him for making me say it. "Suck me," I said, and it hardly even sounded like my own voice saying something so porno. He reached a hand around the front of me just enough to press my stiff cock downward and aim it between my thighs, toward his mouth. He led with his chin and could hardly reach me, but my whole body bucked against the glass when he dragged his lower lip over my cockhead, swirled at it with his tongue, and teased my slit between long, leisurely sucks of the tip.

"Please, oh God. Please do it deep."

He slid his hot mouth from me and then flipped me around, one strong hand keeping me from tripping over the wad of clothing at my feet. "That's right," he said, caressing the side of my cock with his cheek. "I want to look up into your face while you come."

And then my awkwardness increased exponentially as I realized Jacob Marks was gonna stare at me while my cock sank into his throat. He was gorgeous—simply beautiful. The most handsome man I'd ever been with, that I ever even dreamed I'd be with. And yet it was easier to spread myself wide open and half naked on that damn window than it was to look into his eyes.

I closed my eyes and concentrated on the rhythm he set, on the exquisite suction he maintained and the way he opened his throat every few strokes to take me all the way in. But then I heard a murmur of distant laughter—maybe just some tourists on the lake, but maybe not—and I opened my eyes again to keep myself with Marks, anchored in the present, among the living.

I grabbed his short hair, struggling to find something to hold on to, and he grasped me by the hips and sucked hard. My whole body tensed, poised on a painful brink, and then everything crashed open, my hips bucking as Marks rode out my orgasm. His fingers sank deep into my hipbones with a force that'd leave bruises.

Marks pulled off slowly and gave my wet, red cockhead a lingering lick while I stared down at him, dazed. He looked up at me for a long moment, and then kissed it again. And licked it. I pulled back from him, quelling the need to giggle at the sensitivity. "Stop it, Marks. You're killing me."

He sat back on his heels, still fully clothed, and licked his lips. "Why don't you call me Jacob?" he suggested.

Chapter 10

Marks—Jacob, I mean—snores a little. I think I was relieved to learn it. If he was absolutely perfect, I'd have to be suspicious.

I woke around six, and while it would've been nice to get a few more hours in, I was surprised to have slept as soundly as I had. I hadn't spent a night in another man's bed since...I thought back. Maybe eight years earlier. That college professor who was always high—on weed, not Auracel. That was back before they even made Auracel and I'd needed to take Neurozamine with a Benadryl chaser to shut out the voices.

Eight years. I felt old. Jacob mumbled a little, as if my stirring had bothered him, and then rolled onto his back and settled into the long, slow breaths of deep sleep.

I stared at his gorgeous profile and told myself, yet again, that I was actually sleeping with him and that he'd been the one to initiate it. Maybe I'd just been poised for a little good luck. It was about time.

I'd showered and made a pot of coffee by the time Jacob shuffled out of his bedroom in nothing but a pair of blue paisley boxers. "It's seven o'clock," he said, squinting. "Are you crazy?"

"They did treat me for schizophrenia for a couple of years before they figured out I was talking to real dead people," I replied. I'd meant it as a joke, but it'd come out kind of edgy.

Jacob looked me in the eye for a long moment before he sighed and poured himself a cup of coffee. "Well, you're not a kid in an institution anymore," he said. He took a sip of the coffee and winced, then scooped a few spoonfuls of sugar into it. "You're a cop. You can speed. You can carry a gun. You can tell other people what to do and they'd damn well better do it."

Maybe in his world. He was a big, strapping guy with a deep voice and a piercing gaze that could nail you to the wall. I just talked to dead people.

But Jacob didn't see me that way. Psychs were like shiny new toys to him, endlessly fascinating and inspiring. If he felt cheated that he only had access to five senses, he didn't let it slow him down much. And why should it if he could demand the services of two federally licensed Psychs and a suspended cop with the elusive gift of *si-no*?

"Someone told Warwick I was talking to Gutierrez," I reminded him as he speed-dialed Carolyn.

"And?"

"And he said he'd suspend me if...."

"Carolyn? Hey. Let's get together at my place today for some brainstorming. No, you don't have to bring anything. Mmm hm. Yeah, I do have some ideas, but it'll be easier to just show you when you get here. Right. Bye bye."

I got Lisa's number from the Fifth Precinct and convinced her to take a cab over to Jacob's. She insisted that there wasn't much she could do without her gun and badge, but I reminded her that she'd been at the Blakewood scene and seen the victim with her own eyes. We'd just bat some ideas around, I told her. I hung up and looked at Jacob. He had that grin on. Okay, and maybe I was also a little curious about how far *si-no* could actually be taken.

The girls arrived at Jacob's around noon and we convened around a table full of salty Chinese take-out. "So you've played the *si-no* game most of your life," Carolyn said, "but haven't had any formal training."

Lisa nodded. I think Carolyn intimidated her. Heck, Carolyn intimidated me a little.

"We'll need to be careful how we phrase our

reports," Carolyn said. "You're not officially part of this investigation at this time." She looked at me. "Unless you think you can convince Sergeant Warwick...?"

"Not a chance. I thought he was gonna have an aneurysm."

"Fine. Then we'll just need to be aware that anything Lisa says is unofficial. Nothing appears in the report. If her talents lead us to the murderer, fine. But we'll have to scrape together some kind of evidence that could've plausibly led us there besides the *si-no* game. Got it?"

"Carolyn can't simply lie," Jacob winked at her. "The downside to her talent."

Carolyn ignored him and consulted her notepad. "Let's establish some boundaries first." She fired off a series of questions about current events and other factual things to establish a baseline.

"Does Lawrence Avenue run North-South?"

"No."

"Do I have an aunt named Mabel?"

"Yes."

"Has Jacob ever owned a dog?"

"No."

Carolyn looked to Jacob, and he nodded. "Poor baby," she said, the corner of her mouth twitching. He smiled. Carolyn turned her attention back to Lisa. "Am I happy?"

Lisa stared.

"Well?"

"I—I dunno."

"Too broad," Carolyn said, scribbling notes. "Do I like my job?"

"Y-yes."

"You just let me unnerve you—don't worry about it. Not everything can be answered yes or no. Sometimes it's both. Sometimes it's neither. And sometimes the question is just too vague."

It occurred to me that Carolyn would make a good Psych Coach. She was just so nonchalant about it all, and yet you could see she had all eight cylinders firing. Plus, she knew if you were lying. Okay, maybe that part was a little bit scary.

"All right. Let's look at the case. You understand you are here in an unofficial capacity."

"Yes."

"Good. Let's focus on the killer. Is the killer male?"

"Yes."

I thought about the anal penetration and blushed. Lisa knew I was with Jacob. And Carolyn? Jacob said he was out to her. So she probably knew, too, because if the subject had come up at all, it wasn't as if he could hedge. I blushed harder and drank some soda, tilting the huge cup back to hide my face.

"Is he Caucasian?"

"He...." Lisa stared off as if she had to search for the *sí-no*.

"Is he Latino?"

Lisa thought hard.

Carolyn scribbled some notes and then looked up. "Is he of mixed heritage?"

"No." Lisa looked as if she'd surprised herself. "No, he's not."

Carolyn tried a barrage of ethnicities: Greek, Lebanese, Egyptian, every Asian type she could think of, and on and on. Jacob and I chimed in too, but all of our guesses were definite "no"s.

After fifteen minutes of hunting, Carolyn held up her hand. "Let's move on," she said. "We'll wear her out if we continue in a nonproductive vein. She's a resource, not a suspect."

"Unofficially," Jacob said.

"Unofficially." Carolyn turned to face Lisa, her hands on her knees. "Let's look at his history. Has he killed more than two victims?"

"Yes."

"More than two in this city?"

"No."

"Is he intending to kill again?"

"Yes, I think."

"Too vague," I said. "Maybe he's crazy and he doesn't even realize he's killing them."

"Right," said Jacob. "He's so sexy they just die from the touch of his dick."

I felt my face flush so red at that one I had to hide it in the napkin, but Lisa went pale.

"Yes," she said quietly.

"You're kidding," said Jacob. "Yes?"

"There's something paranormal at the heart of this," Carolyn said, mostly to herself, as she jotted some more notes.

"Yes," said Lisa, and I shivered.

Chapter 11

We rested awhile, turning on the news, which nobody watched, and then they grilled Lisa again. I could tell she was getting fatigued, but she's a tough girl and she was willing to keep going with it late into the night.

If we couldn't get an I.D. on the killer from the witnesses, Jacob reasoned, we'd just have to get a look at him ourselves. We narrowed our questions down from, "Is he in the city?" to "Is he east of...?" "Is he north of...?" "Is he on this block?" "Is he in this building?" "This apartment?"

I think even Lisa was amazed at the power of the *si-no* in the hands of a pair of relentless questioners.

"Does he live in this apartment?" Carolyn asked.

"No."

"Is he alone?"

"No."

Jacob stood up. "I think we'd better pay

Casanova a visit. Right now. You go home," he told Lisa. "No gun, no badge—it's safer for you that way." He turned to me. "You riding with us?"

The image of me riding in the back seat like a little kid returned. "I'll...uh...take my car."

Carolyn verified the address with me and I nodded. "Let's go," he said, and we were off.

I turned off the GPS and drove there myself. We headed for the northern edge of Boystown again, not two blocks from the record store where the clerk I'd dated used to work. I wanted Maurice. Or Lisa. Or even to be sitting in that damn back seat. I turned the GPS back on just to have a little company, though since I hadn't entered a destination, its tasteful British voice was silent.

An SUV pulled away from the curb right next door to the apartment building and I pulled in, glanced around, and found Jacob parking across the street. We met up at the gate.

This gate actually locked, unlike mine, but Jacob ran a pocketknife down the edge and it popped right open. We trooped across the courtyard to the far right vestibule, and Jacob studied the apartment numbers by the beam of his penlight. "Here's the one," he said, tapping on the name "J. Barlow." "Get one of the neighbors to let us in."

Carolyn glanced up to see which windows

were lit. "They're less likely to hide from her," Jacob explained. "Strangers don't realize that she's the one they need to be afraid of, not me."

"Ha ha," she said dryly, then pushed a button. A woman's voice said "hello." "Official police business, ma'am. Please buzz us in."

A crackle that sounded kind of like, "...*bzzt*... finally here...called..." came through the speakers and the inner door clicked open. Music with a heavy, thudding beat flooded out.

We jogged up to the second floor and stopped. Someone's stereo blared so loud that I could feel the vibration through the soles of my shoes. Carolyn gestured to me and I bent so she could talk in my ear, not that I thought the suspect would've heard her if she'd shouted aloud. "Loud music—like the first victim."

And maybe the second, for all we knew. The other half of Ryan Carson's duplex had been empty that weekend. That's why it'd taken so long to discover his body.

Jacob scowled at the unmarked doors. We were looking for apartment 2a. But there were three doors to choose from. Was 'a' on the far left or the far right? I touched one door, then another, but they were both rattling equally from the cranked up stereo. Jacob gestured for Carolyn to go with me, then pulled out his gun and approached the left-hand door—the most likely door, in my mind, if the lettering system went left to right like a western alphabet.

Of course, the right-hand door was closer to the stairs, and would be the first door you'd approach. I drew my gun and wished Maurice was there. He wasn't very quick, but he was accurate.

Jacob's hand was on his doorknob and he watched me to make sure I'd do the same. I put my hand on mine and felt the vibration carry right through it. Jacob nodded and we both tried our doors at once. Mine opened. I didn't have time to see if his did or not.

I held my gun at my side, camouflaged by my body. There was no need for the whole, "Police! Freeze!" business since we were acting out a routine noise call, but the thought of coming face to face with the mystery man gave me the creeps.

Carolyn had her gun out, pointed to the floor. She edged to the right, my usual position, so I went left. I passed by the stereo and saw it was on. Framed photos on top had fallen over. I swallowed. I'd picked the magic door—lucky me.

I wished I could turn the damn music down. The beat of generic technopop made my fillings rattle. But at least it hid the sound of our entry and would give us a chance to get a look at whatever we were up against.

Carolyn ducked into a doorway then came out signaling clear. We made our way through a sparsely furnished dining room. I glanced into the kitchen—empty. She checked a bathroom. There was one room at the end of the hall, the door open a few inches with yellow light shining through the gap.

Carolyn held my glance for a moment and then nodded. The bedroom. It was the only thing left. I nodded back and we burst in together, both our weapons drawn.

It was like a bad porno, only I was there, front and center. A dozen candles ringed the bed, lighting the room in a warm, inviting glow. The pair on the bed were kissing while they fucked, and the muscles of the top's buttocks flexed as he pushed in. The bottom was a tanned guy who clearly worked out. He lay back on the bed with his feet slung over his lover's shoulders. The guy on top was tattooed and sinewy, his amber hair cut in a shag like an early-70's glam rocker.

Carolyn stepped back, but I just stared. The tattoos were so strange, colors and whorls, and they seemed to undulate as the man moved, always moving, caressing, thrusting.

He couldn't have heard us over the music. Couldn't have seen us with his eyes closed. Yet somehow I could tell he knew we were there. He raised his head to look, breaking the kiss, and that's when I knew for sure that he was our killer.

Something stretched between his mouth and his lover's. It was thick, viscous, and thinner in the center than either end, like the tanned guy was full of syrup and the tattooed guy was sucking it out. It quivered there between them, glistening and slimy, and then it grew so thin in the middle that it snapped.

I know it was probably there just a nanosecond. But I saw what I saw. When this gelatinous funk snapped back toward the guy on the bed, there was a face in it, a stretched-out, human face. And it looked like it was screaming.

Then I staggered back, sickened by the sight of that ooze, but Carolyn was at my side with her gun leveled at the tattooed guy. "Freeze," she shouted, her voice hardly audible over the music. "Police!"

He cocked his head and looked at her as if she were the most peculiar specimen, and then he looked back at me, and somehow, into me. He opened his mouth.

I didn't want to know what was in there. I tried to look away, but the strength had leeched right out of me. I didn't have enough left to even avert my eyes. I'd rather see anything but that sickening maw. But there it was, filling my vision, opening wide.

He was displaying himself to me, I think.

Showing me that inside him was nothing, an absolute void. Pitch black where teeth and tongue and throat should have been. Flat black and featureless, like a poorly doctored photo. Nothingness had never been so scary.

And then he screamed.

At least, that's the best way I can describe it. It was more like the shriek of a train trying to brake, hitting too many discordant, screeching pitches all at once. Horribly loud, even over the blare of the music, loud enough that it hurt, badly, and I shrank back and covered my ears.

I saw the dresser mirror beside me shatter, rather than hearing it. It was almost beautiful, like snow falling. A thousand shards glittering as they rained against my side.

Then the windowpane blew out, and gauzy curtains fluttered through with the force of the blast, like a gale had whipped up inside the room and sent them streaming toward the outdoors.

The guy with nothing inside him stretched, very quickly, until he was more of a rubbery line than a person. And he was out the window and gone before I could fully register how he'd even moved.

The beat of the music continued to pound through the soles of my feet, but I realized I couldn't hear it. My ears were still ringing from the sound of that metallic shriek the killer had made before he'd disappeared.

Carolyn was beside me, tugging at the sleeve of my sportcoat, but I was just too stunned to acknowledge her. Then she was gone and the music stopped reverberating, and the quality of the sonic aftershock changed somewhat in my own hearing. And then Jacob was there, shaking me by the shoulders, hard. "Vic," his mouth said, judging by the shape of it. "Vic."

I tried to focus on him. I think he was clutching me so tightly he might've actually been hurting me, but I didn't really care. Then Carolyn dragged him toward the bed and he left me there, leaning back against the closet door, standing amidst a spray of broken mirror.

Chapter 12

The sun was up by the time I was coherent enough to talk to Jacob. The paramedics said I was in shock. Jacob had done CPR on the tanned guy, one James Barlow, until the paramedics arrived, but it had been no use. James was victim number three—in our city, at any rate.

We lingered in Barlow's courtyard, well away from the plainclothes officers and the techs who were starting to swarm the scene. "I couldn't hear anything over that music," Carolyn said. "But Vic held his head like he was getting split in two."

"All right," Jacob said. He pulled out his notepad. "So what did you see?"

"Well," Carolyn said, "the men were...together. Having intercourse. And the man, um...well, the killer, looked at us and opened his mouth, like he was yawning. And then the mirror and the window shattered and he was gone."

Jacob wrote very quickly. "Okay. But what

did the killer look like?"

"Caucasian. About forty-five. Short hair, salt and pepper. Brown eyes."

Jacob frowned. "That's nothing like the other descriptions." He turned to me. "Is that how he looked to you?"

I shook my head. "Thirty, maybe less. Tattoos." I felt myself color. "Actually, I thought he looked like a young David Bowie."

Carolyn looked away. "George Clooney," she said.

Jacob's eyes narrowed as he considered Carolyn. "You got a thing for George Clooney?"

Carolyn scowled at Jacob as if he was a jerk for even asking. "Don't tease me."

"I'm not. I have a theory, and I know you can't lie to me if I ask you something directly. So. Do you?"

"I think he's attractive, yes."

Jacob looked at me. "David Bowie fan?" He wasn't making light of it, not in the least, but it still felt too personal to divulge that Bowie'd been my biggest masturbatory fantasy until I discovered flesh-and-blood boys who were willing to experiment with me.

I thought of making a snide remark anyway, but I figured if Carolyn could admit her crush, I could admit mine. "What she said," I echoed.

At least Jacob gave me the courtesy of not verifying my truthfulness by double-checking it with Carolyn.

"So our killer looks different to every person who sees him, tripping some part of the witness' neurological wiring and showing him or her the image of someone they consider to be extremely attractive," said Jacob.

Carolyn considered. "And so a majority of people are going to see the killer as someone of their own ethnicity. But different ages, different particulars. We haven't asked any of the witnesses whether or not they thought the suspect was attractive. But it might be a promising line of questioning to pursue."

Jacob stifled a yawn. "We've been at this more than twenty-four hours straight. I suggest we get some sleep and regroup at the Twelfth around two. That sound good to everybody?"

Carolyn was halfway to her car before I'd even had the chance to agree. Jacob blocked me with his body before I could follow. "Stay with me," he said, so quiet I almost couldn't hear him over the residual ringing in my ears. Or maybe it was my brain.

Relief washed over me, but it drained away as I realized that I really didn't want Jacob to see me that way—spooked by some killer psychically disguised as David Bowie who sucked souls out of men while he fucked them. Because that was the only thing that syrupy stuff could've been. A soul.

And the killer'd gotten too much of it before we'd arrived, and now James Barlow was on his way to the Coroner's.

"I really need to change my clothes," I said, squeezing past Jacob as I tried to recall where I'd parked.

Jacob fell into step beside me with a couple of long strides. "Then stop at your place first and then come over. You don't look so good."

I neglected to say that I had to buy a jacket, actually, since both of mine had doubled as splatter guards in the past two days. Damn the police department's dress code.

I found where I'd parked and we approached the spot. "Two o'clock," I told him, got into my car, and shut the door. I wouldn't say he looked hurt standing there beside the car while the morning commuter traffic flowed behind him. But his self-assured grin was nowhere in sight, either.

I pulled into the stream of traffic and gave the finger to some jagoff who honked at me. I'd wanted to stay with Jacob. In fact, I was kind of blown away that he'd even asked. But I felt like what I'd seen earlier had soiled me somehow, and taken a lot of the parlor-game fun out of my talent. And if Jacob figured that out, I'd go from being creepy and fun to just plain old creepy in his eyes.

I wasted a good twenty minutes getting to

SaverPlus, only to find it didn't open until ten, and it was barely nine. Not having another hour to waste, I headed home and took a shower. I wish I could say it was a long one, but there just wasn't time.

And then I got into bed and closed my eyes. I'd been kinda scared that I might keep seeing that black, empty mouth again, the hole that led to nothing. But I could summon up images of lake skylines and whatnot to keep it at bay.

The ringing in my ears was another thing entirely. I got back up and swabbed them out with Q-Tips, which changed nothing. I found a pair of earplugs in the back of a drawer and put them in. The ringing changed in pitch, but also seemed to intensify. Finally, I turned on the radio, desperately seeking something other than asinine morning DJ banter. I found a Spanish language station, which seemed okay at first, if a little chipper and bouncy. But then a commercial came on and it was so jarring it nearly blew me out of my bed.

Finally, I flipped the dial until nothing but garbled noise came through, popped a Seconal, and passed out.

Two o'clock was ancient history by the time I woke up—two o'clock in the afternoon, at least. It'd be two a.m. in about fifteen minutes. Shit.

I checked my cell phone for messages. There were only a couple, both from Jacob. From two-thirty: "Vic. Your input would be helpful on this report—but if you can't make it until tomorrow morning, that'd be fine, considering the shock. I let both of our Sergeants know what the paramedics said. We've got Archives researching to try to figure out what this thing is, based on Carolyn's statement. Give me a call." He left his home number.

And then, from nine: "It's me. Look, I hope I wasn't out of line this morning. I just need to know that you're okay. Call me."

I decided it wouldn't be worth waking Jacob up just to tell him I'd overslept, so I texted him a note that said "SRY I MISSED U, WERE OKAY" It occurred to me that "we're" looked more like "were," but I was too lazy to find the apostrophe. I wondered briefly if SaverPlus was open at two a.m., and then considered that perhaps the shock hadn't worn off yet. My ears still rang, but just a little, and I turned on the white plastic 9-inch TV in the living room to drown it out. Infomercials.

Aside from the obvious concern in Jacob's voice, the thing that stuck with me most was the idea that he and Carolyn thought they could put a name to this thing, this seductive souleater with a big, empty void inside him. And what if they could? What if it was actually some sort of known entity—and what if there was some sort of method or charm we could use to stop it?

Each apartment unit in my building had a storage locker in the basement, behind the coin-operated washing machines. I kept my textbooks from Camp Hell down there. I figured I might need them someday, though I didn't want the evil I associated with them in my living space 24/7.

As I dug the basement key out of my kitchen junk drawer, it occurred to me that maybe I could wash the marinara off my new jacket. It was from SaverPlus, after all. Maybe it was made out of indestructible, machine-washable polyester. I checked the label. Wool blend. Dry clean only. I wondered how bad it'd be if I machine-washed it anyway. And then I realized that since I didn't own an iron, it probably wouldn't do me any good to even try.

I felt naked venturing down into the basement without a load of laundry to protect me. The narrow, dark stairs were a lot creepier at 3 a.m. than I'd imagined.

I stepped carefully to avoid pissing off whoever else lived in the building and made my way down into the cellar. The part that housed the furnace and hot water heaters was closed off with some newish looking drywall, but the exterior walls were nasty, old limestone slabs with crumbling mortar and greenish mildew between. A bare 75-watt bulb shone scant inches from the top of my head, but the unfinished wooden floor joists above it were so dark that they seemed to eat the light. Kind of like the mouth of a certain creature whom I was absolutely not going to think about until I was safe and sound in my white apartment with every single light turned on.

A gurgle sounded to the right of me and my glance snapped downward. I flinched back, thinking, "Rat!" But the thing that had caught my attention was barely visible, faint bluish lines that I had to squint to make out against a dark concrete floor.

And then it came together all at once. A spectral baby, fists flailing, with an umbilical cord still attached.

Jesus. Someone'd left a newborn to die down here. It could've been a month ago, it could've been half a century ago. I didn't care. Humankind just sucked. If I had a bottle of Auracel in my hand I would've downed the whole thing in hopes of never seeing another fucking revenant.

I stepped over the baby's ghost and unlocked my storage unit, too disgusted to try to keep quiet any longer. I let the metal door bang open and yanked out an old nylon gym bag. How many times had I stepped over that damn baby and never seen it? It'd probably died somewhere around 3 a.m. and that's when its presence was the strongest. Damn it all to hell. I was gonna have to start using a laundry service.

I stomped back up toward the first floor. A door swung open on the landing and a guy in a robe came out to see what all the noise was about. He stepped into my path, but then recoiled and shut his door. I guess I must've looked pretty pissed off.

Once I was back in my apartment, I turned on every damn light and left the TV going, tuned to a station I don't receive so that it played nothing but a staticky white glow.

I've never been booksmart, and I didn't pay much attention to what they tried to teach me at Camp Hell unless it brought about immediate relief. And nothing had really done that except pharmaceuticals. But I remembered enough, if I pressed myself, to recall that there was a section on paranormal creatures in one of my texts.

Vampires were the first thing that came to mind, but the two main categories I found were blood fetishists and psychic vampires. Since there'd been no blood at any of the scenes, maybe our killer was a psychic vampire, and that stuff I'd seen stretching between him and the victim was some kind of ectoplasm. I followed that line of thinking, about how the vampire was charismatic and seductive, and if he or she sapped a victim long enough, the drained person would eventually weaken and die.

Except that didn't make sense. The book said they'd die, not be utterly destroyed. It was a gradual thing, not the result of a one-night stand. And the thing we were hunting didn't just drain people of energy. It ate their very essence.

My eyes felt sandy. I closed the book and rubbed them, which made them feel worse, and went into the bathroom to see if I had any eye drops. I stopped in front of the mirror and stared hard, making sure the guy looking back was actually me.

Sure, my hair was a mess, as usual, and I was working on three days' worth of stubble. But my face itself was a wreck. Tiny red lines crosshatched my cheek, some crusted with dried blood, others just there, bled out. And my eyes were something from a bad horror flick, the whites all red with burst blood vessels. I'd always gotten some attention for my frost blue eyes, especially since they were set off by my black hair. But the red...it was a whole new look for me. Jacob had invited me over looking like this? Boy. He really did like his men creepy.

That'd teach me to let mirrors explode on me. But my eyes—crap, that thing must've burst the blood vessels in my eyes with his scream. I shuddered and twisted open the eye drops, only to discover they had evaporated, leaving nothing but a tiny, plastic bottle crusted around the tip with salt.

I watched the sun come up, then went to the drug store and grabbed some eye drops and sunglasses. After that I stopped off at the cleaner's, only to determine that they kept items no longer than 90 days. I left them to deal with the marinara sauce, and then sat in the parking lot of SaverPlus until they opened.

I bought two sportcoats. Both black. Tore the tags off and threw one in my trunk, put the other one on.

Everything I needed to do had taken a lot longer than I'd thought it would, so I figured I'd better let Jacob know I was on my way. I peered over my sunglasses into my rearview mirror while I waited for him to pick up the phone. The part of my eyes that was supposed to be white was blood-crimson, even more hideous in natural light than it'd looked in my bathroom. No wonder Jacob had sounded worried.

I got Jacob's voicemail. "Hi," I said. "I'm running a little late this morning, but I'll meet you over at the Twelfth. Unless that's not where you're gonna be. In that case, call me." Boy, was I slick or what?

As I pulled up alongside the Twelfth, I

realized that I could've called Jacob earlier instead of sitting outside SaverPlus twiddling my thumbs. I could've called Lisa, too, and filled her in. Sonofabitch, why was my brain such a sieve?

I walked out and shifted my jacket, thinking that either I'd grabbed a different style or accidentally taken a 42. At least the sleeves were long enough. As I blew by the front desk, one of the plainclothes officers peeled out of his regular spot to intercept me. "Detective Bayne?"

I stopped and turned, and wished I didn't feel the need to wear my cheap new sunglasses inside. Between them and the overlarge jacket, the cop probably thought he was having an 80's flashback. "Yeah?"

"Sergeant Warwick called. He wants to see you at the Fifth Precinct."

I felt myself sag inside. I used to coexist peacefully with Warwick, but lately everything he said to me made me cringe. Or maybe it'd been Maurice who'd actually gotten along with him all these years.

"Okay. I'll just touch base with Detective Marks...."

"He's not here. I think you really need to see Sergeant Warwick."

My blood curdled in my veins as I wondered if something had happened to Jacob. I hopped in my car and slapped the police light on the roof, doing ninety all the way to the Fifth Precinct. I barreled through the front doors, up the stairs, past Betty's desk and into Warwick's office.

He stood up and glared at me. "What's with the sunglasses?" he demanded. "Are you on drugs?"

I stopped and stared, flabbergasted by his question, but too scared to challenge it. "Where are my partners?" I asked him. "Have you heard from them?"

"Marks and Brinkman are at the Commissioner's office, giving their reports about the murder scene you discovered last night."

"Oh," I said, and my heartbeat slowed. "Okay. Good."

"But they're not your partners anymore."

"What?"

"You're off the case. In fact, you're suspended." He tapped on the desk with one thick, callused finger. "Your badge and your gun."

"Suspended? What for?"

"I warned you not to leak information to Gutierrez—and who did you run to the second you left my office?"

I gaped at Warwick, wondering who could've possibly told him we'd gone to Gutierrez for help. Could he have a wire tap? Someone tailing her? Wouldn't he need a court order for any of that?

Whatever he had on me, I had no idea how to talk around it. I put my badge and my gun on his desk, thinking that I'd always imagined it would feel worse to give them up. It felt like nothing, like paying for the sunglasses or asking the pharmacist about eyedrops.

It felt mundane.

"And just so you don't get any bright ideas, Gutierrez is in police custody."

"You arrested her?" My voice cracked.

"She hasn't been charged with anything...yet. But the two of you are through playing psychic telephone."

"What the...? You can't just hold her. She can sue you. I hope she does."

"And then she and I can discuss the consequences of all those tests she cheated on."

Shit. I wished I was up on my legal rights, but I'd never even considered that I might be suspended. Never even known anyone who was.

Warwick sat down and took my badge in his palm. I thought maybe he looked regretful as he stared down at it, but what did I know? My eyes hurt. "Go home and get some rest, Bayne. You look like shit. Let Marks handle it."

"I need to give my statement," I said, grasping for some way to keep hold of the investigation.

"I haven't given my statement."

"I'll tell Marks. But for now, Vic, just go."

Chapter 13

I was glad that voicemail doesn't register hang-ups, because then Jacob would know that I called him approximately every ten minutes, although I only left him one message where I stammered something about being really sorry that I wasn't at the Twelfth like I'd said I would be, and that my text message was supposed to say "we're" and not "were," but that I was feeling much better and I really wanted to see him. I somehow managed to keep from apologizing for even being born. Barely.

As I thumbed through my Camp Hell textbooks yet again, I wished that I'd made a friend or two there, someone I could call and ask, just theoretically, what kind of supernatural beastie sucks out people's souls while they screw.

And then it hit me. A succubus.

I flipped my book open to the index and found a half dozen references to it.

Succubus: Lascivious female demon who takes the form of a comely young lady; said to possess mortal men as they sleep and to sup on their essences. According to one legend the succubus and her male counterpart, the incubus, were fallen angels.

Sup on their essences? I glanced at the date of the text and found it was written in 1964. Queer. And not in the way I like. None of the other passages were particularly enlightening, either.

So it was possible we were dealing with... what? A gay incubus, or a male succubus? Maybe. If I could just get in touch with the archivists at the Twelfth, I could give them my impressions. They had access to stuff that was written sometime after the dark ages, unlike me. Even databases. They'd know the latest research on entities that used to be called demons.

Because there had to be some sort of modern take on the demon. Red men with pointy ears and pitchforks: unlikely. Powerful psychic beasties that could pop all the blood vessels in your eyes by hitting the right note? Well, we had to call it by some name, and incubus was as good as any.

But I was off the case. The archivists at the Twelfth probably couldn't even talk to me. I glanced up at the clock. It was nearing seven p.m. They would've gone home by now anyway, I told myself. And I called Jacob's cell phone again.

"Marks."

"Oh! It's uh...you picked up."

"Hold on." I heard him cover the phone with his palm and excuse himself. A moment later, he was back. "Thank God, Vic. Are you okay?"

"I'm fine. But Warwick took me off the case."

Jacob's voice was an urgent whisper. "It came down from the Police Commissioner. They've been going over my statement with a fine-toothed comb all day. It's out of the bag that we used a psychic without a federal license to locate the crime scene, but I think that since we caught the guy in the act, they're gonna find a way to let it slide."

"But what about Gutierrez? Warwick said she was in custody."

Jacob sighed. "I can't talk now—this place is crawling with the Commissioner's elite officers. Meet me where we had dinner on Tuesday and I'll fill you in. Same time."

"Okay. But, Jacob...?"

"Gotta go. See you then."

In an attempt to clean up, I went into the bathroom and started shaving. The shaving cream stung as I smoothed it on, and even though I opened a new razor, it seemed to keep catching on scabs and hunks of dried blood as I dragged it over my cheeks. By the time I was through, I came to the realization that the stubble would've looked much better. And then I stuck a dozen little bits of toilet paper to my face. I wondered if SaverPlus sold welding masks.

I had half an hour to kill, so I got on the phone with the Fifth and tried to call around and find someone who could tell me where they were holding Gutierrez. An older cop who worked the night desk, one of Maurice's friends, told me she wasn't there—but that was as much as he knew.

Too bad I didn't have a touch of the *sí-no* or I would've tracked her down myself. But what did I have? I was a fifth-level medium. That was almost as high as you could go. There were a few level-6s scattered around and a single level-7, an old lady in France who could actually command spirits. But she'd died in her sleep a couple of years back and become one of those spirits herself.

So I could hear, and sometimes see, the dead. And they seemed to sense it and be sure they talked my ear off. Thing was, they never knew shit.

I needed to get going to make it to the restaurant by eight, so I slipped into the goofy new blazer and set out. The GPS managed to lead me, yet again, into the worst snarl of traffic I'd seen since the time I was late for a root canal. Eventually, I crept by an accident.

A couple of glowing blue spirits gawked from the side of the road, but since they were dressed like they'd come right out of an off-Broadway production of Grease, I figured they weren't a result of the accident that they were rubbernecking.

I turned down an alley, out onto a main thoroughfare and picked up some real speed. Maybe Jacob would know where Gutierrez was. He'd help me get her out, or at least get me in there to talk to her, tell her it was gonna be okay.

I got to the restaurant ten minutes late, a miracle considering traffic, and didn't spot him anywhere. For once I wasn't the latest one. The maitre d', a thin Midwestern guy with steely gray hair, seated me. I wolfed down a bread stick, and then another, and then I realized that I hadn't eaten anything yet that day.

Eight twenty and still no Jacob. I ordered an iced tea. I flipped open my phone and tried his number, just to gauge when he'd get there. Maybe I could start with an appetizer. Maybe I could even finish it before he got there and order another one like I hadn't just inhaled one by myself. I'd have to pick up the check then, but fair is fair.

His cell went directly to voicemail. "Hey, Jacob. It's Vic. Let me know how long you're gonna be. I might need to start without you. Bye."

I ordered some soup—nothing that would stain my blazer too obviously—and scarfed down half the bowl. Jacob was probably talking to his sergeant, or maybe to Carolyn. Had her statement been taken separately from his? Likely, since the three of us had come up looking fishy. In retrospect, I was glad I'd overslept.

The iced tea caught up with me, and I flagged the maitre d' over so that he could tell Jacob I was there, in case he showed up while I was in the bathroom, which Murphy's Law said he would. "White male, olive complexion, six two or three, well built, black hair, brown eyes, short goatee."

The maitre d' frowned in thought. "One moment," he said, and flipped open his reservation log. "Jacob Marks. He was here earlier, sir. He left."

"Shit! Uh, sorry. How long ago?"

"Shortly before you arrived."

"Did he leave a message for me?"

The maitre d' shook his head. "I'm very sorry." He turned to greet some new customers that had walked through the door, but I caught him by the sleeve.

"Did it seem urgent?" I asked him. "Was he on his phone, in a hurry?"

"I'm sorry," he repeated, and turned toward the customers.

I grabbed him more forcefully and wished to God I had my badge. "Look. I'm a cop, and this is police business. What else can you tell me?"

The maitre d's eyes showed white all around. "He left with someone. A young man."

"What did he look like? Describe him."

"I...I don't know."

"Height, weight, race, hair color."

"Thin. Athletic. Blonde. He looked a little bit like Brad Pitt, actually."

Or maybe he looked an awful lot like Brad Pitt. And George Clooney and David Bowie. I hardly remembered letting go of the maitre d'. I was back in my car with the flashing light on the roof and absolutely no idea where I was headed.

I fishtailed into traffic and tried to think. Every crime had happened at the victim's house. And there'd been one every night, or every other. The incubus got around.

I swerved down a side street and headed toward Jacob's. I shut the GPS off and then flipped open my phone. "Information? Connect me to Carolyn Brinkman." Electronic noises came through as I begged that her home number was listed. "Douglas and Carolyn Brinkman," the computer voice said after an excruciating pause. "To connect, press or say one, now."

"One," I barked, and after some more weird, muted digital sounds, Carolyn's phone started to ring. "Thank God," I said. "Pick up, pick up, pick up."

Instead, a man answered. "Hello?"

I swerved around an overturned shopping cart that was laying in the road for no apparent reason. "Carolyn—I need to speak to Carolyn."

"Who is this?"

"Detective Victor Bayne. It's an emergency."

"Look, Mister Bayne, I know things look bleak, but you've got to see it from Carolyn's point of view. She's sorry about what happened, but it wasn't her fault. The poor woman can't lie."

"What? Yeah, I know about her talent. But I've gotta talk to her. It's about Jacob."

"She's finally calmed down enough to get some sleep, and she's on enough Neurozamine to obliterate The Amazing Kreskin, so she's not going anywhere tonight."

Jesus H. Christ on a bike. Coolhand Carolyn had doped out on us. Shit. That was usually my department. Jacob had told me on our first day together that Carolyn never took meds. I assume she hadn't been lying to him, considering Carolyn's double-edged talent.

"Look...ah, I get it. I'm a Psych, too."

Her husband sighed. "Then you know how hard it is. I'm sorry, Detective. But this business with Jacob will have to wait until tomorrow."

"Can I at least come and get her gun?" I asked. But the line was already dead.

You'd think I would've had some reason to buy a gun other than my service weapon during the last twelve, fifteen years. Then again, you'd think I owned more than one or two sportcoats, too. Shit.

But I knew someone who did have a gun, someone I'd been dying to see. I hit memory dial one, Maurice's cell phone.

"Hallo." A crowd noise swelled around Maurice, and I tried to imagine him among a sea of humanity, but couldn't place where he might be.

"Where are you?"

"Fort Lauderdale. Don't you remember? I told you on Sunday. I'm at the casino."

Shit. Oh shit. No. He couldn't be in Florida. I needed him here.

"Good thing you ain't a precog or I wouldn't even be able to talk to you in here. Nichelle just won five thousand nickels on a slot machine. You believe that? That's only two hundred fifty bucks, though. You say five thousand nickels, it sound like some huge jackpot."

The first vacation Maurice has been on

since his fucking honeymoon and I call him, hardly able to restrain myself from begging him to hop the next flight home. What good would it do, other than spoiling his good time? It wasn't as if he could get back here any sooner than tomorrow morning. And by then it'd be too late.

I tapped my brake as I flew through a stop sign. "Look for a slot machine with a...a star," I said, pulling a psychic prediction out of my ass even though Maurice and I both knew I was about as precognitive as he was. "And don't let anyone know I told you."

"A star, huh?" Tinny ringing, jingling noises filtered through the murmur of the crowd. "You're all right, Bayne."

"Gotta go," I said, and hung up before Maurice could figure out how stressed out I was. The fact that he could barely hear me had worked to my advantage, but I wasn't gonna push it.

How much of a lead did Jacob and the incubus have on me? Maybe half an hour, but maybe less. They were probably driving like normal humans, not like me. I turned onto Jacob's street and swung into a spot by a hydrant, bumped the car in front of me and left the rear end of my car sticking out at an angle as I ran toward Jacob's condo building for all I was worth.

As I wrenched the vestibule's outer door open, a low, thudding vibration tickled the base of my skull.

Technopop.

Chapter 14

I nearly rang Jacob's doorbell and then realized he might not be able to answer. I rang every neighbor's bell instead. "Police," I shouted to the first one who answered. "I'm here about the noise complaint."

They buzzed me right in.

Some little part of me must've been holding on to the hope that Jacob wasn't really with the incubus. That all the clues I was seeing—that he'd left the restaurant with Brad Pitt, that the same inane electronic beat buzzed through the floorboards of his condo and out into the hall—actually added up to something else. But when I put my hand on his doorknob and the door swung open, unlocked, my stomach clenched up and I felt numb all over. Because the unlocked door was just like every other scene.

I took in the entryway, the broad living room and the archway leading to the kitchen in one glance. Jacob's jacket was in a pile on the sofa, and his holster lay on top of it.

I grabbed his gun.

The stereo was right there. I could've turned it off and bought myself some space to think. The incubus probably already knew I was there, or would know before I had a chance to blow it away. But something about the music seemed inevitable, like I needed that throb to shift myself into the incubus' plane well enough to kill it.

They'd be in the bedroom. Because that's where all the other victims had been. I ran full-tilt toward the bedroom door, because if there even was a remote chance that I hadn't yet been detected, that damn music covered the sound of my approach. I held the gun at face level—none of that vertical-beside-the-head stuff you see on TV. That fucker took Jacob, and I was gonna nail him right between the eyes.

I hoped they weren't too intertwined. I'm not all that good of a shot.

I rounded the corner and—thank whatever powers there are to thank—the incubus was in the midst of peeling off Jacob's shirt. He himself was still fully clothed. Jacob wasn't moving on his own, but if the incubus hadn't gotten to third base with him yet, I still had hope.

If it was possible, the creature looked even more like David Bowie tonight, as if my brain had had a chance to peg him into some sort of category and was going all the way in reassuring itself that he fit. He was Ziggy Stardust, down to the glittery spandex outfit and the lightning bolt on the cheek.

"Freeze," I said, in a voice that would've sounded firm and clear in a normal situation. The music totally covered it, but I had a feeling the incubus could filter things like that out. "Police."

He looked up at me and started a little. Maybe he hadn't known I was there. Maybe I could've gotten right on top of him and squeezed off a few rounds before he'd been able to turn into spaghetti and fly out the window. Shit.

With just his head turned toward me, he started to open that black, empty mouth of his. I pulled the trigger. The shot sounded like a pathetic snap that hardly carried over the blaring music. I hit him...I think. I didn't see any blood, any bullet holes in either him or the wall, but he thought better of pulling that sonic scream crap on me again and turned to face me fully.

Jacob remained limp on the bed. I didn't have time to watch him and see if his chest would rise and fall, but I told myself he was just asleep—some kind of psychic trick the incubus had managed. Because the texts said that incubi struck while their victims were asleep, and damn it, something in that worthless book had to be true.

The incubus saw me glance at Jacob and smiled. His lips were closed, stretched over the blackness even more thinly. He reached toward Jacob. I squeezed off another round, aimed at his arm. A black bullet hole appeared in the wall behind him.

Ziggy Stardust thought that was funny. He stretched his arm closer to Jacob, going in slow motion to savor my reaction to it all the longer.

I was getting nowhere fast with the gun. I didn't fling it aside or anything melodramatic like that. Heck, I might still need it. But I used another weapon that I supposedly had in my arsenal, at least according to Camp Hell.

I shot a blue bubble of protection from a space between my eyes and above, a little outside my physical body. Third eye, pineal gland, seventh chakra, it's all the same. When you're psychic, it's where all your weird shit lives.

The bubble was so strong I actually saw it. Maybe nobody else would've, but I saw it in the same way I'd seen the dead baby in my basement or the spirits hovering around the accident. It sealed Jacob up tight. I let go of it, and it stayed there.

Take that.

The incubus saw it, too. He poked at the bubble and it stretched a little, but held. He looked back at me, his eyebrowless forehead hitched in the middle to show me his displeasure. He grabbed at Jacob more forcefully, but his hand glanced off the bubble.

I knew what I needed to do. Send him toward the light. I took a deep breath and then shot a sphere of light out toward him. It encircled him like a psychic spotlight, glowing beautiful and pure.

He touched it, and it shattered.

He smiled, showing Bowie-esque teeth a little square and crooked, but I could still feel the blackness lurking there behind them. "Aren't you just a breath of fresh air?" he said in a melodious English accent, his voice carrying effortlessly over the grinding cacophony of the electropop. "And what's that little trick you just tried to pull?"

I leveled the gun at his face.

"Now, now. Why so jumpy? I just want to talk. There's no harm in talking, is there?"

Probably. I didn't give him the satisfaction of a reply.

Instead, I made another white bubble, and I imagined it was a hundred times stronger, swirling with layer upon layer of psychic energy, impenetrable. And I flung it.

It engulfed him, pearlescent white whirling around him like a cloud cover. It held for a moment. And then it shattered.

"How did you do that?" it asked. "You're mortal. I can smell your soul. Come on," he coaxed, easing forward, "Let me get a better look at you."

I backed up a step. That was a good white bubble, a damn good one, and yet the incubus was just too strong for it. It was a stupid idea anyway, trying to scare off a demon by putting him in a bubble like Glenda the Good Witch. What I needed was a house to drop on him.

He took a dainty step forward, then another. "You don't need to be afraid," he said. "We'll just get to know each other a little better. I can make you feel very, very good. You're such a fascinating chap—I promise I won't kiss you until you grow tiresome."

He was on me now, his pale, slender hand reaching toward me. I didn't know how I'd respond to physical contact with him, since it was possible he'd trip some psychic synapse in me, maybe short me out. "Your pickup lines need a lot of work," I said, and then I pulled an image from the cop portion of my brain. I imagined something black, thick and suffocating, a shape that was man-sized, yet vague and featureless. I wrapped him up in a psychic body bag and zipped it up tight. And then I imagined it was totally lined with mirrors and sent that idea blasting toward him.

He just stood there for a second while

I waited for him to shatter my shield. He flexed and wriggled, but my body bag stayed solid. I poured more energy into it, imagining the mirrors inside showing him a hundred thousand reflections of himself, except maybe there really wasn't anything to see, only blackness. He let his sonic scream rip, and the bag muffled it and made it even more shrill and ugly, psychic feedback. And I poured strength into the body bag until I started getting lightheaded.

And then I emptied the whole clip into it.

Chapter 15

There was no body to recover, just a bunch of stringy slime—which analysis found to be inconsistent with human remains. And though I'd left twenty bullet casings scattered in an arc around my feet, only a single bullet was recovered, the one I'd aimed at the incubus' arm. That one had lodged in Jacob's bedroom wall.

Jacob's condo was now a crime scene. I'd invited him to stay with me and he'd accepted, though he was still too groggy from the incubus' sleep-whammy to shuttle me to and from the eye doctor's. I'd been about to call another cab for my trip home when Lisa called my cell phone and offered to pick me up.

Lisa waited right outside the clinic, idling in a little red hatchback. She'd walked right out of lockup and bought herself a used car. Not quite the reaction I would've had to incarceration, though she'd had the *si-no* to keep her company, while I would've gotten a dead serial killer hanging by his shoelaces for a cellmate.

The clinic's automatic doors whooshed open and I stepped through, blinking against the glare of the sun. The ophthalmologist had dilated my pupils to look around inside my eyes, and he'd told me the residual blood in the whites looked much worse than it actually was and it wouldn't affect my vision in any way. I made him look inside again just to be sure. They say if you lose your sight, your other senses increase. And if my sixth sense got any sharper, I'd probably kill myself by tripping and falling on it.

Lisa gave me a big grin and reached to turn down the Mexican radio station as I climbed in. "It's okay," I said. "Leave it."

She ignored me and left the volume low anyway. "What do you think of my car? Is it haunted?"

I grimaced and took a quick look in the back seat before I buckled myself in. "Nope. Sorry."

"I didn't think so." She pulled away from the curb and swung around the U-shaped arc of the driveway, slipping into traffic with an ease that made me think she was learning her way around just fine. No GPS unit strapped to the dash. Maybe the *sí-no* was a more accurate way to travel anyway.

"I had a hard time deciding," she said as we idled at a red light. "I think I started out asking the *si-no* the wrong questions. 'Is this car gonna last me five years?' I got a 'no' on everything, and was starting to think the lot was full of lemons." She put her left turn signal on and crept into an intersection. The oncoming traffic showed no gaps, but she waited for the end of the yellow light without any trace of anxiety and took a smooth turn just before the cross traffic gunned into the intersection. "Then I started worrying that maybe I was gonna be crippled in five years, not able to drive a car. Or maybe even dead."

I looked out my window at the line of orderly brownstones we passed. I didn't trust myself to attempt a reassurance that'd probably come out awkward and make things worse.

Lisa waited for a moment, maybe giving me some time to respond, and kept going when I didn't. "I talked to Carolyn. She told me I was reaching out too far. That I should ask questions like, 'Does this car have any mechanical problems?' Or, 'Will I enjoy driving it?'"

"Makes sense," I said. I noticed the leaves on a maple coming up were starting to turn gold. One more year just passing by.

"She's real sorry about leaking our plans to Warwick, you know."

I sighed. "Yeah. I know. I told her it wasn't her fault."

"When Warwick asked her what we were up

to, she didn't even answer him, did you know that? He suspected, though, and when she wouldn't say whether you were talking to me or not, he just took it as a yes."

"I get it. I just said it was okay."

Lisa pulled into a space a couple blocks south of my apartment building. I assumed the *si-no* had told her there wasn't anything closer. "She thinks you hate her now."

"Jesus. I don't hate her. It just scares the shit out of me, how it happened. The thought that Warwick could use her own powers to manipulate her. The idea that maybe someone could do that to me."

Lisa cut the engine and slumped back into her seat. "Yeah. Me too. That's why I think I'm gonna get some training."

I swung around to grab her and shake some sense into her, but the seat belt caught me by the neck. I swore at it and clicked it open, but by then I'd calmed down enough to stop myself from acting like a lunatic. "Did Warwick talk you into it? He probably believes that fucking brochure that Heliotrope Station sends out, but lemme tell you...."

"Vic," she said quietly, putting her hand on my knee. "Calm down. Not Camp Hell. There's a new place in Santa Barbara. It's called PsyTrain."

I hated PsyTrain instinctively, but since I'm

not precognizant, my instincts weren't worth much. "Sounds like a fucking disco locomotive."

"The department will pay for it. And when I'm done, I'll have a job waiting for me."

So that's how Warwick had talked her into it. He'd let her keep on being a cop. Shrewd fucking bastard. "Visit this PsyTrain first before you go," I said. "More than once. And make sure you talk to some people that've trained there, lots of them. And not just the ones they recommend, either. Find some on your own and...."

"Don't worry. Carolyn's going with me to make sure they're honest."

I didn't suppose Lisa could do any better than having the human lie detector in tow, but the mere thought of Camp Hell had sent adrenaline pumping through my veins and I think I wanted to keep on arguing just for the sake of it.

"If something doesn't feel right, I'll back out of it," Lisa said. She gave my knee a squeeze. "I promise. But Jacob's waiting for you. He's worried about your eyes. You should go tell him they're okay."

I swallowed back the urge to bicker and opened the car door. I hadn't told Lisa my eyes were okay—but she knew. I wondered how long it would be before HMOs started scooping up psychics to cut down on the cost of medical testing, and then slapping them with lawsuits whenever their diagnoses failed.

One last look at Lisa's back seat reassured me that the hatchback's former owners weren't along for the ride, and I gave her a brief, sullen wave as she cranked the Mariachi back up and pulled away from the curb.

I could've said something like, "Hi honey, I'm home," when I came in, but that would've implied that I was in a good mood. Which I wasn't.

My futon looked strange, small and a little bit cheap, with Jacob on it. He sat there in plaid pajama pants, hunched over the glass-top coffee table, shirtless and insanely buff, poring over one of my old textbooks. I suspected he'd already read the one about Psy-ethics. He looked up as I came in, his finger marking the spot on the page where he'd stopped reading.

"My eyes are fine," I said. "They just look bad. But they'll clear up in a week or two."

Jacob smiled his broad, infectious grin.

"I'm, um...gonna go lay down," I said, and ducked into the bedroom. Part of me wanted him to follow and help me blow off a little steam. And part of me was drained and exhausted and just wanted him to stay put. I guess I'd get my wish either way.

I kicked off my jeans, pulled on an old pair of sweatpants, drew the curtains and slipped into bed. A few minutes later I felt Jacob's weight settle behind me. "So tell me about this third eye," he said.

I managed to not turn it into a dirty joke, since he was so earnest and all, and I didn't feel much like joking anyway. "What about it?"

"Does it feel like an actual eye to you? Does it blink? Did the incubus' scream affect it, too?"

"It's all a metaphor," I said. "It's not a real eye."

"But the text...."

"Is incredibly hokey and inaccurate. I used to think it was translated from Russian. They had a handle on Psych stuff a long time before we figured it out here. Them and the Chinese."

Jacob eased his arm around me and spooned my back into his chest. We fit our bent legs together, and his knees nestled behind mine. "I know you think I'm pushy for asking...."

"What? No, no I don't."

"I can tell. You sound disgusted when you answer me. But you're a difficult man to get to know. And I'm only trying to understand."

I felt bad. Just a little. "Look at the part on chakras in one of the newer books, the one with the guy on the cover who looks consti-pated. That's a little better explanation."

I think the cover model was supposed to be expressing some sort of psychic talent in action, but I'd always wanted to slip him an Ex-Lax. I half expected Jacob to leap out of bed to go find it since he was so into the whole Psych thing. But instead he just snuggled tighter into my back, his breath warm against my shoulder blade.

And his stiff cock hard against the back of my thigh.

All I had to do was reach back and take it in my hand, let him know that I was ready if he was. And yet I still felt peevish and out of sorts. He sighed and pressed a little harder, his fingertips fanning over my ribs as he held me. I felt a flutter of arousal at his touch, and his warmth, and the sheer solidity of him.

And yet.

Jacob pressed his mouth to my ear. He had a sexy voice and he was shameless about using it. "Make love to me," he said.

I turned my head toward him and his mouth covered mine, the light bristle of his short beard scraping at the criss crossed network of fine scabs on my cheek. His tongue traced my lower lip, drew my tongue out to meet it, but only reluctantly. I knew the incubus had used heavy psychic stuff to seduce him. Call it a glamour, or some kind of mesmerism. But I couldn't help it. I was jealous.

I turned my mouth from his. "I don't have any condoms or lube," I said, and did my best not to count the number of years it'd been since I'd dated someone steadily enough to need such things. The record store guy. Too many years.

Jacob's mouth went to my throat, and he traced a long lick down the sinew of my neck. "Who says I need them?" he asked, and I could hear the smile in his voice. "I just want to touch you. Taste you. Hold you."

His hand skimmed up my body and his fingertips found my nipple, took it firmly this time, and squeezed. Arousal surged toward my groin as if the two points were magically linked, and then he gave a little twist that made me whimper.

His lower hand slipped palm-down beneath the waistband of my sweatpants. My breath shuddered out, but I bit back the moan that threatened to escape me. It wasn't fair that he could make me so hard so fast. He cupped my balls with his palm and twisted my nipple again, and I writhed against him, feeling his hard cock settle in the cleft of my ass.

"Ready to lose the pants?" he asked me.

I wanted to give him a sulky answer, but he was stroking the skin behind my balls, just one fingertip, light and repetitive, and it was like all of my awareness surged into that one spot, leaving me helpless to reply.

He twisted my nipple again, and I arched and moaned.

"God, you're so hot," he said, and sank his

teeth into the meat of my shoulder while he took his upper hand and jammed my sweats down around my thighs.

More shocks of arousal traveled down to my cock, which seemed very happy to be free and butting against the comforter.

I felt him against my lower body, thick black body hair, belly, groin and thighs, tickling against my ass and the backs of my legs. He pressed one of his knees between mine and spread my legs from behind. His thigh was so muscular and solid it felt like iron, and my back arched some more to allow him to spread me.

His lower hand slipped deeper between my legs, fingertips gliding feathery touches over my asshole that left me gasping.

"Touch my cock," I demanded, and my voice was a desperate rasp.

Jacob let go of my nipple and ran his upper hand down my ribs. He gave my cock a cursory stroke, then fondled my balls.

"Goddamn it," I said, but I wasn't mad, not really. Just so hard that it hurt—and he knew it.

His upper hand slipped around back to my ass, spread the cheeks while the fingers of his lower hand continued to swirl and tease. And then I felt his balls nestle against my ass, his thick, hard cock cradled again between my ass cheeks.

"Squeeze," he said, and I clenched up a little. He slid his cock within that cleft and shuddered against me. "Oh, God, yeah."

His voice was thick, not the usual controlled purr I'd come to associate with Jacob, the hottest cop in the city. And I dug that I could do that to him, make him all trembly and needy and hard.

He took my cock loosely in one hand while teasing my ass, my balls, the creases of my thighs with the fingertips of the one he'd wedged between my legs. It would've tickled, except he shifted his grip on my cock and gave it a long, hard stroke.

I arched and swallowed down a yell that would've carried to the next apartment if I'd let it out.

"Like that?" he said, gravelly in my ear.

"Fuck, yeah."

He pulled on my cock again, this time slipping a finger inside me.

I arched, hard, and stroked his cock with my ass.

He grunted and bit down on my shoulder, and pulled my lower body roughly against his on the downstroke. We caught a rhythm somehow, me grinding and clenching the length of his cock between my ass cheeks, him fingering me, stroking me, tearing at my shoulder with his teeth like some kind of beast.

I broke first, grabbing at the comforter, the windowsill, Jacob's wrist as he jerked off my cock, fingerfucked me, his leg between mine opening me even more, spreading me, taking my body and dragging an orgasm out of me.

I gasped his name as I came, my whole body twitching helplessly on his, splayed out wide like I'd been stretched on a giant rack.

He stopped pulling my cock and just held me for those final few twitches, so violent they rattled the bedframe against the floorboards.

"C'mere," he said, once I managed to draw a normal breath. He scootched back and helped me to roll over and face him. He took my trembling hand between his and wrapped it around his cock, and I felt my own come, sticky between his fingers. He moaned when I grasped him, and pressed his forehead into mine. He let go of my hand and brought his fingertips to my face, tracing the line of my cheekbone and jaw while I re-learned the shape of his thick, veined cock, learned how he shuddered when I thumbed the ridge under the head, learned how he groaned when I bore down hard on him and glided strong, even strokes down the length of him.

His top leg was thrown over mine and I felt his thighs begin to tremble as he got close. I slowed my strokes and he hissed, whether in approval or frustration, it was hard to say. And then his fingers wove into my hair and he pulled me forward into a slow, deep kiss as his breath hitched, and his hot, wet come painted my hand, belly and chest.

He kept on kissing me, long after he'd gotten off, until finally he drew his tongue into a gentle sweep across my lips, and he lay back just a few inches from my face and sighed.

I held him and felt his breath warm on my cheek, the weight of his leg solid and heavy just above my knee. It was so close to perfect. Except for that cold knot in my belly that told me my jealousy was still coloring everything.

"It's none of my business," I said, "but I can't help but wonder whose face that incubus was wearing for you. I mean, who's so great that you'd ditch me at the Cottonwood Lounge and run home with him?"

"You're kidding."

I closed my eyes so I didn't have to see him looking at me and decided it was best to keep my mouth shut, too.

"You are kidding, right?"

As if I would make a joke about something like that. I kept my eyes closed and refused to answer.

Jacob's sticky fingers traced the shape of my face yet again. "You really don't know, do you?" He pressed a gentle kiss onto one of my eyebrows, then the other. "It was you, Vic. He disguised himself as you."

About this Story

It's unfortunate that I can't write at the speed of thought. When I first started writing this series, Victor Bayne was about my age...and now I'm catching up with Jacob and not-quite-forty Vic has been looking more and more like a young whippersnapper!

Among the Living was written in answer to a call for entry for a novella-length story featuring paranormal beings in everyday situations. I hadn't really thought about writing a series back when I got the idea for PsyCop. It just seemed like it would be an interesting premise to have psychic cops going around doing their jobs, but then also dealing with the personal ramifications of being psychic, because certainly, the knife needs to cut both ways. It's no fun giving a character a supernormal power without also saddling them with a liability that's just as prominent.

The worldbuilding and characterization were the two things that made me eager to keep expanding the PsyCop world once this initial story was written. It seemed like there were so many more profoundly awkward situations with Vic's name written all over them just waiting to be explored.

I don't think PsyCop should go on forever, since series that do that, in my opinion, tend to overreach the protagonists' character arcs and jump the shark. But thanks to the world-building I've done so far and the slow but sure evolution of my narrator, I do have at least a couple more PsyCop stories planned before Vic will need to ride off into the sunset.

Victor Bayne considers himself a one-trick pony, just an unfortunate guy who sees ghosts. But it turns out he's got another talent up his sleeve. Continue your PsyCop adventure with Thaw, a heartwarming PsyCop short. Available free on JCP Books in ebook and audio.

JCPbooks.com/ebook/thaw

About the Author

Jordan Castillo Price is optimistic enough to hope that psychic powers could be real, and cynical enough to assume that someone will undoubtedly exploit them should tangible evidence of the sixth sense ever become incontrovertible.

Before she was an author, Jordan was a screen-printing salesperson, a graphic designer—and briefly, even a secret shopper. (Yes, that job does exist.) In Chicago, she stitched her way through an MFA in Fiber Arts. She now resides in Madison, Wisconsin.

More Stories